I0699625

Praise for The Bad Blessings

"I appreciate Sotelo's vivid realism, supernatural intrusions, and eruptive interplay of interior monologues...."

-Dr. Jon Hauss, Professor of English; American Literature and Literary Theory

California State University, Dominguez Hills

"An anticipated novel for Latinx readers"

-The South Gate Chronicles

"The Bad Blessings is not only about the experiences of a queer child; it is also about childhood itself and its accompanying confusions, questions, and poignant discoveries."

-Dr. Nishant Shahani, Associate Professor; Women's, Gender, and Sexuality Studies

Washington State University

"This story grapples with the common adolescent challenges of self-discovery and longing for freedom while growing away from one's home yet trying to maintain strong family ties."

-Dr. Sarah Minslow, Assistant Professor of Children's & YA Literature

California State University, Los Angeles

"Beautiful imagery; Sotelo has a unique ability to capture emotions with a swift sound of words...."

-Long Beach Review of Books

"A story like [The Bad Blessings] simplifies complex philosophies and questions about life. It makes them relatable and applicable for our everyday life."

-First Circle Books

"Magnificent, didactic yet simple. The Bad Blessings dazzles the minds of young readers and inspires reflection in all readers…."

-San Francisco Literary Cafe

The Bad Blessings

By

Everth Sotelo

First Circle Books

First Circle Books, 2022

The Bad Blessings

Copyright © 2022 by Everth Fernando Sotelo Munoz

All rights reserved. Published in the United States of America by

First Circle Books, Los Angeles, in 2022.

Library of Congress Registration number: **TXu 2-339-774**

Cataloging-in-Publication Data is available from Library of Congress.

ISBN: **979-8-9872718-0-3**

First Hardcover Edition, 2022

Text set in Adobe Garamond

Printed in the United States of America

To all those who supported me…

Life is not a problem to be solved

but a reality to be experienced

-Soren Kierkegaard

1

The mare's wails itched my skin like crawling ants. She twisted and struck the wood off the paddock, and my throat tickled from the cloud of dust. The farm was dead-silent, except for the agonizing wail of the mare. Pa, as I called my father, ordered me to look away. But it was hard to turn my rebellious gaze from her horrible pain. Pa injected a thick syringe into her buttocks, and the mare's pain subsided. His forehead was soaked in perspiration. Pa's old friend and owner of the estate, Thomas Estrada, a wealthy businessman in the food industry, rushed out of his house filled with anguish.

"Will she be, ok?" He muttered.

"She should be fine; let's allow nature to do its work," Pa said.

Thomas wiped the sweat off his eyes. That mare had been bred to produce a rare colt. He only trusted Pa, the only veterinarian in Amourville, to deliver such an elegance. The whines resonated over the ranch; my stomach was a whirlpool. Pa approached the mare with caution. He gently ran his fingers through her flank and whispered to himself. Thomas glanced at Pa, desperate for a response.

Pa nodded with a grin, and then they stepped away to observe the miracle. A black circle appeared on her genitals, like giant red lips. The lips grew bigger and bigger as the mare quivered, then a few drops of liquid oozed out. My eyes squinted at the bursts of fluid. The hoofs enclosed in a milky sack stuck out. The mare shook and squealed, and the sack continued to squeeze out. Finally, she got her front legs up, and the movement pushed the sack out a little more. The baby horse hung from her. I wanted to pull the foal out for her. I hated to see animals in pain. Why was life so painful? My saliva turned salty, and my stomach swirled upside down...the ranch was getting blurry.

Alice, Thomas's wife, a slim girl with lyrical blue eyes, porcelain skin, and jet-black hair, pulled me towards her. I took a deep breath, and the blurriness went away. She was so lovely; too bad she was older. We could have been great friends, but she was my best friend whenever we visited the Estrada's.

"Stay here; we can't disturb this special moment," Alice said.

"Special? It's painful!" I replied.

"Such is life."

"Will she die?"

"I hope not."

"Is life painful?"

"Not really, well, sometimes, yes." She pulled me closer to her skirt.

Where does pain come from? I didn't understand the concept of pain or why people cried so much. But this birth taught me that it's just part of being human. Pa taught me that being independent and acting upon my principles would protect me from life's pain. Anything that makes me not me is pain. He was wrong, to a certain extent. Poor mare, perhaps she did not want to have a foal. Kids were never for me. No way, too much pain and commitment. I wanted to be just me.

The mare jerked faster, and as her bones crunched, my hairs rose. The milky sack wobbled out of her, and then it got stuck! Pa gently pulled the bundle. She shrilled, and the sack finally gushed out her hole and spilled a puddle of liquid. The foal's little head ripped through the thin sack, and Pa cut the umbilical cord. Thomas rushed to admire the white colt; he was speechless.

A hot and cold shiver rushed through my vulnerable body.

"Come see the foal, Rose!" Pa said.

Alice pushed me towards him. Each step became heavier, but I needed to know if the mare survived.

"You can't pet them right now. The mare is very protective; just watch." Pa said.

The colt gazed at me with the ocean in its eyes. It was like she was making a connection that would mark me forever. The colt blinked......

Are you in pain? I miss Ma,   *I don't know*
why I came!   *Why is it looking at my eyes,*   *like*

all over Amourville,   people see me everywhere   even in   the church,   there is God's eye, but these aqua eyes hold energy, a thought, a warning   when is dinner? I need to get some sleep before we leave,   poor mare, it hurts, I know it hurts,   you probably did not want the baby you deserve freedom, Ma I wish you were her but this feeling, it is great,   this little horse   it talks to me... we will see each other soon under the worst circumstances   and I'll be there to save you...   the little horse spoke to me, it spoke to me! Yes little horse, I hope to see you soon, welcome life is not that bad you will see......

I pressed my face against Pa's leg. My teeth would not stop chattering. Finally, the mare turned toward the shivering foal and gently licked it.

"It's a big risk to initiate a new life; that's why we must enjoy life as much as we can," Pa said.

"What?" I asked.

"He means we should be happy for the foal!" Alice said as she took me by the hand.

Pa stayed behind to chat with Thomas. Thomas's smile, all too larger than life, left no doubt that he loved the little horse. But I hope the mare no longer feels pain, a pain I always dreaded.

After that tumultuous day, Alice helped me pack for our return home. Pa's practice was in the big city, but we moved to Amourville when things got too expensive, or that's what he told me. He then did veterinary services in smaller communities and traveled a lot. I was 7 years old, and

I loved to travel with Pa. There was always something new to experience, unlike when Ma took me to church or when Kashmir would nag. Pa's travels led me to see the world. One day I will get out of Amourville and fulfill all my dreams. But the mare's labor was my first encounter with reality, the complete shatter of my dreams, but then I understood how much pain it takes to simply live.

Our travels to the Estrada ranch were always fun. Alice was like an older sister I never had. I don't know why Kashmir has always competed to be better than me, but she was always detached. Too bad Alice was married. I don't think she liked it. She responded to Thomas by saying, *yes sir*, and bowed. He yelled at her, too, like Pa yelled at Ma......

No man will ever tell me what to do   I will not lose who I am; that's pain   I will never get married   not to a man   women are more angelic.   I just feel like   like…they are more loveable   more beautiful   I better finish packing......

Alice's father died when she was a little girl. Her mother worked as a seamstress but could not support her seven children. Her father worked in construction in Willicha, the town next to the estate where Thomas met him. Alice's marriage was arranged to support her mother and siblings. I would be devastated without my family, especially my beloved Pa. She did not love him, or it seemed like she didn't. They were hardly together. Pa seemed to talk to her more. I'd rather die alone than marry only because we have no money. I could say she taught me that love is an absolute illusion that controls you; that is why I am here. Alice then showed me how to fold clothes. I had a lot to learn in life.

Pa came to check on my packing progress. Alice bowed her head, and I ran to hug him. Pa examined my luggage and was surprised to see the neat arrangement. Alice kept her face down, and Pa continually exchanged glances between her and me. She stepped out of the room, and Pa completely ignored my excitement. He asked me to finish and went after Alice.

My eyes squinted over the pages of my favorite book. The voices in the hall kept me from sleeping. Pa and Alice never returned, and my curiosity ran wild. There was a deafening silence in the dark hallway. My fingers stiffened at the touch of the cold walls, which were the only tangible thing in the darkness. The lights flickered, and my heartbeat was rapid. My gasps resonated in my ears. But then, ghastly murmurs echoed at the end of the hallway. The murmurs came from Pa's room, his door was not closed completely, and a dim blue light reflected from his room. The murmurs turned to familiar voices that gasped for air, and curiosity led me to peek inside, but......

No! Ma told me that even a cat's sleep was sacred
    Papa is probably too tired   but what if he is choking,
I got to help him!   No ,   I have to sleep
    my eyes burn and... and...   I
can't wait to be back home,   I miss Ma,
    those moans sound a bit painful   Papa must not
be ok   the mare poor thing   a God that allows pain like

that must not be a God   what is this?!   Ok, ok   just a little peek   why must I be so curious   it   will   be   really quick   Pa is probably just missing Ma   he must miss her   my throat is so dry from the air   after all this I need water   water   poor mare needed water   what is this? What are they doing?......

Pa was on top of Alice, their clothing was on the floor, and their moans intensified. My body was frozen, but my innocence was gone; that's how people do it. My fists tighten. I smiled, but the urge to punch someone ran through my fists. That was jealousy; I was jealous that she was with Pa.

A door squeaked at the end of the hallway. An ominous silhouette stood at the end of the corridor. I walked towards it---not knowing that it would change my life forever---my eyes could not move away from this image, "Rose…Rose…Rose," it whispered. There was a creepy door at the end of the hallway and darkness in every direction. The door opened slowly with a hair-raising creak. There was pitch darkness inside, except for an old light bulb above the frame. An old woman with yellow eyes, a white gown, a necklace with beads resembling eyes, and a blue turban stepped out. She lit a candelabra shaped like a hand and held it in front of me. The stone hand had a carved pale eye with stars; the eye sparkled and grew larger and larger. My body was frozen, the eye, the eye, it petrified me. It has been looking at me until now…

A strange mumble came from her puckered lips. She rotated the candelabra counterclockwise around my face and chanted. The old woman then moved around me, hysterical and creepy.

My legs were noodles, my forehead beaded with perspiration. I did not know what she was doing, a spell? A knot tied around my throat. Then, finally, she stopped and blew out the candles. Her face floated in the darkness and told me:

"Bring me your blood…."

I ran back to my room. That was the scariest moment in my life. To this day, goosebumps and tears overtake my body just by the thought. Who was that woman?

Alice woke me up. It was now time to leave. The bars of sunlight moved across the floor from my bed. I could see the outside world, ready for me. I just kept thinking… perhaps it was all a nightmare; at least that was my consolation. The birds chirped and my impatience to leave pushed me out of bed. That experience changed my life. Little did I know it was not over.

"Your papa is waiting for you!" Alice said.

Alice helped me get dressed. She wore the same clothes as yesterday. At that moment, I wasn't clear about what they had done, nor had I had the courage to ask her. A deep confusion stirred in me: Should I like her or hate her? Now the answer is clear, but innocence protected me from revenge.

"I missed you last night?" I said.

She remained silent as she combed my hair. Her expression was sullen and serious.

"Please promise me one thing…." She stared at my eyes in the mirror.

"When you find true love, don't let go of it, no matter how hard it is. It may never come back to you." She whispered.

"Are you in love?" I asked.

"Yes…" She replied.

Pa called for us from the hallway. Alice closed my luggage and left the room without accompanying me. It was like Alice had changed. Was love making her mean? She left a cold impression on me, but the fun was over.

Thomas loaded our luggage into a red Jeep outside their big house. I ran to the paddock where the mare roamed with her white colt……

There was no hate within them   these   animals show   love and care   why does pain have to exist in such a lovely world?   Some   milk   sounds   good   right now   what was that   last night   and why was Pa with Alice?   I should tell Ma   or maybe not   I wish I could be that horse, free, without anybody telling me   what   to   do   enclosed   in   a paradise   oh yeah that's what everyone calls Amourville the city of love I feel lonely there   I would love for Alice to come with us   is Alice in love with Pa?

is that how it will be when I fall in love?　　　　　Uhh!　　Love!
I want to be a mare, free　but if Alice loves Pa, then who does Pa love?
Ma?　　　I want to love whoever I want　　　　whenever
however!......

We all gathered around in front of the house for a family photo. The woman from the night before hovered out the house like a ghost. She carried a camera and asked us to pose. Pa got close to Alice, but Thomas pulled her by the arm towards his body. Pa stood next to him, and my feet were immobile. The witch-or so she seemed like one-sneered at me. My reaction was to bow my head, but Pa pulled me by his side. Alice frowned, and she rolled her eyes at me. The drastic change confused me. Either she was mad at Thomas or jealous I was next to Pa; the moment was awkward. The witch set the timer and ran to pose next to Alice. Pa patted my head and asked me to smile. It was hard to pretend. My choice, however, was to smile, for my Pa at least.

Pa placed me into the back seat. Alice stood a few feet away, about to burst into tears. It felt unlikely that any of us would see each other again. The woman grabbed her arm and pulled her to the veranda. She looked at Alice with disdain, then the woman locked eyes with me. Her eyes were darts that ripped through my flesh. Her deep demonic voice whispered in my head that she wanted my blood. The more I looked at her, the higher the pitch of her voice. Pa shook me, and I snapped out of that trance. We waved bye and drove off. A close distance grew between Alice and me. Her figure dwindled as the Jeep accelerated, and fear tangled up my spine, fearing that her frown would haunt me for the rest of my life.

At the harbor, my father pulled me out of the Jeep. The gentle breeze cooled my balmy skin and ruffled my dress. Thomas gave my father a hug. He then went to his knees and hugged me.

"Be brave," Thomas said.

My eyes widen……

the mare   blood on his arms   the   witch rotating the hand   Alice's sinister stare   yes   I will be brave,   I know I must be brave, but why did that woman do that, why did Alice change?   Who is she?   Is this pain?......

Why did he say that? I did not know, but he had a point; that trip taught me to be brave and realize that pain was inevitable. Pa picked up our luggage, and we walked to the tail of the ticket line. Thomas stood by the Jeep with a sad expression. Pa pulled me by the hand, but I could not help but look back at Thomas. The crowd of people erased him from my sight. Perhaps it was not him whom I missed. I miss that red Jeep; maybe one day, I will have one like that.

Port Granada was the hub of commerce. Tourists roamed its docks like ants in a colony. The rotten smell of fish gagged my throat, and seagulls sang in the skies and blocked the walkways like gatekeepers. The tumultuous voices were rocks that rolled inside my head. Port Granada had boat routes through El Coco River, an ocean-like river that linked the coast to the inland. It was an alternative to car travel from Amourville or the big city, which were at least a day away. The ginormous ferry sat on the water like a fortress, unmovable and scary. But the delicious smell of hot dogs pulled my face away from the metal monster. A kid stuffed his face with the grilled sausages, and my stomach yelled at me harder and harder. Pa didn't buy me one. I hated to depend on people. But I learned that when I want something, I should be able to get it, no matter what. Pa gave me a piece of cardamom bread. All I wanted was to leave that place.

Ahead of us stood twin girls around my age. They gave me the friendliest smile ever.

"What is your name?" One of them asked me.

"Rose," I said.

"I am Lea."

"I am Lisa."

They wore purple dresses with white bows on their head, and their leggings were white with shiny black shoes. Both had ebony eyes and bob hair and faired skin. They looked like caricatures, and I was taller than them. The twins invited me to see the fish in the river. Pa looked at his watch.

"Just for a bit. We will leave soon." Pa said.

The twins took me by the hand, and my eyes spun like wheels as we zig-zagged across the labyrinth of voices.

We arrived at a secluded shore of El Coco River. My eyes squinted at the sparkling water, and the breeze refreshed my dry entrails. The twins sprinkled water on each other. A wall of water lifted me towards the sky. Higher and higher, until the water wall held me over the pastures, on the unseen side of the river. The flowery meadow kissed the blue horizon, and the cotton-weaved clouds, dropped by the gusty wind, hung over the haze of the city's skyscrapers. Little angels flew around me, waving their hands. They pointed down, and my stomach swirled. The mighty river divided the infested port from the pristine fields. The little angels laughed……

I can feel   I can feel   I can feel
nature   How beautiful is it to be free, in
nature   Yes, it's nature the one that brings freedom
but   if God created nature, then how come we are not
free?   I want to stay up here   Pa   must be
worried   I better get down before the ferry leaves,
I want to stay here where its free,
nobody tells me anything   why does the water take me
here   because it knows what my heart wants
nature loves me   and   I   just   I
am a bit hungry   want to   be part   of
nature   how can I solve the pains of life?……

The water wall brought me down to the pebbly bank, and the angels waved as they ascended to the skies. The river was then filled with yellow butterflies. They gently tapped into me as they rose towards the sky. As the yellow cascade passed, I saw a rainbow, and a light protruded from my heart. The rest of the butterflies flew into the woods.

I ran over to join the twins, but something caught the corner of my eye. An old fisherman navigated a boat with the help of an ill-complected boy. He gazed at me with a faint smile. The twins shouted, "he likes you!...... You got a boyfriend!" He waved, but my response was to crinkle my nose like the stench of rotten fish. As their boat rowed through the river, he could not take his eyes off me. Boys did not interest me, at least not romantically. I grinned but never waved back. Their boat disappeared at the end of the river.

I ran to join the twins. Lisa handed me a bag of breadcrumbs to feed the fish. Then, as the drops fell, the fish swam around our feet in circles.

"Are they kissing?" I asked.

"They are fighting for food," Lisa said.

"But they do kind of look like they kiss," Lea said.

"Yeah, but I wonder how they tell who boys are and who are girls," Lisa said.

"Imagine kissing girls!" Lea said.

"Ehh!!" They both said.

"I don't think they care. They all just seem so happy!" I said.

"That's true. Animals are always happy." Lisa regarded.

"That boy was cute!"

"I don't know. He was scary." I said.

"I think he likes you!"

The twins laughed. My eyes turned to the fish to dissimulate. While the twins laughed at my rare encounter with this boy, I wondered, who decides who I should love? Society? My family? Or me? The boy was nice, but there was more to love than just a boy. Why must I like a boy? There was a lot to love in nature. Nature loved me. The twins couldn't stop saying how much they wished to be with a boy. Some girls were just boy-crazy. I hoped that one day I would like a boy. But I was still unsure about who I wanted. Finally, the ferry's horn thundered across the port; it was time to leave. We plodded out of the water, and the twins took me by the hand back to the dock.

Father was speaking to someone from the crew. The twins ran back to hug their parents, but Pa's expression carried disappointment. The crew member gave him the tickets back, and he went on his knees to speak to me.

"We must stay here tonight; the ferry is full."

"But Ma will be worried. I don't want to stay, Pa."

"Sorry, love, but it will be fine. I'll call her." He said.

"Can I say bye to my friends?" Pa nodded.

The twins stood in front of me, filled with joy. I stepped into nature because of their friendliness. But it was bittersweet to say bye.

"It was so nice to meet you girls," I said.

"Where do you live?" Lisa asked.

"In Amourville"

"Really?! We live in Solvang, close to you. Maybe one day we can meet to play!" Leah said.

"Yes, we can be the circle of happiness like the fishes!" I said.

"The fierce three!" We all laughed.

Lea handed me the bag of breadcrumbs.

"For next time we get together to be happy." She said.

I took the bag, and my eyes became a little teary. The twins taught me that friendship is the essence of love, and that love began in nature. We gave each other a group hug, the last sincere hug of my life.

The ferry's horn made the final call. The girls ran to their parents and waved at me from the ferry. The gate closed, and smoke puffed out of the chimney. The passengers faded into a cloud of smoke with shades of red from the majestic sunset in the back. The smoke dissipated, and the boat was gone.

Pa and I walked into the streets. A sword stabbed my chest as a woman with several children begged for money. How could life be like this? How could I have everything and these kids nothing? My impulse was to somehow help the poor woman, but Pa pulled me away and told me not to worry.

"Make the right choices, and you won't end up like her." He said.

I thought God would help her make the right choices. But later in life, reality struck me that we make choices, not God. But perhaps it was not her fault; maybe her husband chose for her. No man will ever choose for me.

We entered a moist alley with a stench of rotten eggs and dim blue lights suspended from wires. There was trash all over, and rats crawled around some trash bins. It was dark without any hope at the end. The crowd became rowdy, and my fear was to stay on those streets. Pa held me against his body, and we entered the black alley. The furor of the street dimmed behind us. Pa's steps were slow yet sure. My heart was beating rapidly. There was a white dot at the end, and my vision blurred as my face cluttered against Pa's leg. The white dot amplified, revealing the port's other side. Cans rattled from the wind's howling blow, ominous whispers traveled in the air, shadows hovered in the dense fog, and my stomach swirled at the only sight of life, an old inn. We rushed over, and the urge to pee overtook me.

Pa knocked on the office window and scanned the area. The parking lot was packed without a soul in sight. An old man with a stern look opened the window.

"Do you have a vacancy for two, just one night?" Pa asked.

The old man scanned and stared at both of us. He then nodded.

"Can I see the room first, please?" Pa pointed his head towards me, and the old man sneered at us.

We climbed up narrow spiral stairs. The rusted handles rattled, and the stairs could have crumbled down at any moment. The old man arrived at a room, swiveled his keys, and slowly opened the door for us, Pa, and I peeked in.

There were three beds. There was a young couple to the right; they seemed foreign. The couple peeked their heads out of their quilt and looked at us with discomfort. Across from them were two men. It was the first time I saw men kiss. They kissed passionately, like two people in love, isolated from the world, which was beautiful. The men waved at us. We would have slept between these couples, but Pa refused the offer.

"Pa, why can't we stay? I am tired," I said.

"What those beasts were doing was sick and wrong. God will destroy them!"

"Why? They are happy…"

"No! Men belong with women! And a woman should always be with her husband! Understood!"

"Yes, daddy."

But my reality was different……

<table>
<tr><td>they were happy,</td><td>nobody should tell you</td></tr>
<tr><td>who not love</td><td>why do we like God's love but not other</td></tr>
<tr><td>people in love?</td><td>It was just beautiful,   they did not care</td></tr>
</table>

*why were they hiding, probably from people like Pa
I am getting tired need to sleep   poor men   I wonder if the
twins have reached the end of the river,   they were so much fun!
                    How would it be to kiss a girl?   If I am in love
then it would be lovely, oh but no Pa said that was bad, don't want to
get him mad!   Maybe it is wrong, God made us just right
                    but   I am happy they make
their own choices   why always with my husband…   I don't
understand,   no Pa, I don't want to marry, I want to play   but
what if I want to be alone   Pa seems anxious…   yeah
he is tired   he loves everyone he is just tired   but not
scared, Pa is never scared   should I ask?   Its best I don't think
about it……*

"I wish you could have been a boy to beat up all these gays."
Pa said.

          *……A boy, then if that is what my Pa wants then, yes I can
be anything I want, boys kiss girls then that makes it right?
No?   I just want to go home   but I need to pee……*

Pa's body disappeared in the ghostly-gray fog. All I
could feel was his damp hand keeping a grip. In the howling
silence, there were spine-tingling voices. Then, a yellow light
appeared in the distance. We kept walking until the fog
dissipated. It was the port's food stands.

"Are you hungry?" he asked. "No, I need to pee," I said.

          We passed the stands until we came across a logging
house much smaller than the last place. Pa knocked on the

door, and an old woman opened the door. As soon as Pa asked for a vacancy, she welcomed us inside.

Despite the cozy appearance, the house was a gothic castle, where imagination was unnecessary to believe in the uncanny. The old woman opened a room and extended her hand to invite us in. It had one small round window, a bed with a thin mattress, and an antique desk and chair. Although compact, the woman stepped in to turn on the lamp. It cast a dim orange glimmer.

"The bathroom?" Pa asked.

"I was going to bring you a bucket. Sorry, it's outside, but please don't go out." She said.

"Why?" Pa asked.

She gave no answer and stepped out. My skin cringed as I sat on the cold bed, but my feet thanked me for the relief. Pa hunched to prevent his head from touching the cracked roof. The woman peeked in and handed him a bucket.

That night I had a terrible stomachache. No matter the position, the pain would not go away. Pa touched my forehead and neck, a fever boiled inside me, and my stomach pain was sharper. Pa left the dark, cold room in search of the old woman. An uncontrollable shiver took hold of my body. The moon hung over a black gradient, ghastly scattered clouds surrounded the orb, and the ethereal glow shined into the room. My pain would then come and go, but my eyes were on fire.

Then a spine-chilling squeak tickled my ears. It sounded like a cart. The squeaky wheels came closer and closer until it stopped, and a horse whined. When my pain lessened, I peeked out the window. A dilapidated cart strode into the moon's glow. The cart hauled chained bony figures, and their laments echoed across the street. The driver turned his face towards me with a ghastly pang and stared at me with two red eyes.

My pain returned with a vengeance. The shadow's red eyes tightened my throat, but I couldn't scream. My legs couldn't hold me, but light rays emanated from my belly. An orb with wings detached from me, and my stomach pain was gone. The orb giggled like a child, illuminating the entire room. The shadow outside melted by the light, and my body glowed. My stomach pain subsided. It was so painful that I thought I would die. Suddenly, Pa grabbed me from behind. The room was dark again, the orb was gone, and my pain returned.

Father placed a freezing towel on my forehead. The old woman stepped into the room. She poured olive oil on my stomach and gently rubbed it in circles--the earthy fragrance was pleasant. Their voices echoed in my ear for a moment, but when they clarified, she said the nearest doctor was about two hours away. Pa looked hesitant, but my pain began to subside. She kept rubbing my stomach until there was no pain. The old woman touched his back and smiled. She stepped out, and Pa flipped the towel. My body felt cooler.

"Pa, will we ever see Ma and Kashmir?"

"I hope so."

"Will I die?"

"No!"

"But if I die, then what is the point of life?"

"You are not going to die."

"What if I just do! Tell me, daddy!"

"There is no point to life…you just need to be happy."

"Then I want to be a lawyer! Defend all the girls from mean boys!"

"That's good, my love! Do what you want. No matter what, always remember to love yourself."

"Yes, daddy. Is life easy?"

"No, it is a big problem."

"Can I fix it?"

"One day, maybe."

"Pa, what's wrong with me?"

"I am not sure, maybe something you ate."

"Will we leave tomorrow?"

"Depends on how you feel. If not, then we will go to the hospital."

"Pa, does the devil exist?"

"No, why?"

"Then why is there pain?"

"Because of choice…" he leaned towards me, "man is God's mistake, and man created the devil in fear of blaming God." He whispered.

"Then God is bad?"

"We are all good and bad. Now get some rest." He laid next to me.

My eyes were as wide as a valley……

Will I die tomorrow, or right now?   I don't want to feel pain anymore   so if God made us and then we made the devil then   did   God   create   the   devil   too? Oh Ma! I miss you   going to church with you is boring but   now   I want to go   ok everything is God's fault   why create a devil?   Umm, umm   fear? Fear of God?   Why fear someone who is good?   I don't understand   maybe it's all a lie   maybe Pa is right I   love myself   I want to go home please pain don't come back will I ever see home again?   can't keep   my   eyes open……

The morning rays tickled my eyes. Pa combed his hair, and my eyes gazed all over the room. I thought it was another nightmare. He kissed my forehead and took a fresh pair of clothes from my suitcase. Pa stepped out of the room, and I jumped out of bed to look out the window. A swarming colony of people against a peaceful blue sky, birds chirp, and a foghorn vibrated the thin glass. There was no explanation for last night's visions. It was best to get dressed and leave. Pa knocked on the door, stepped in, and picked up our luggage. Outside the lodging house, the old woman sat on her porch as she knitted with the utmost care.

"That is so nice," I said.

"It's a face mask. I feel it in the air; a pandemic will hit us soon." She said in a somber tone.

"What is a pandemic?" I asked.

"When the world dies a little more…." She whispered.

Pa yanked me by the hand before I could ask another question. We were in a hurry, and Pa would not have had an answer anyway. Some things are best left unexplained. As life became more complex, things revealed themselves little by little in the strangest way.

We were among the first to board the ferry that morning. The crisp wind froze my frail body as we climbed to the top deck, but Pa's hugs kept me warm. The deck was a melting pot. It was frustrating yet exciting to listen to different languages. It wasn't like Amourville; dull and antiquated. Only English and some Spanish are spoken, one religion, one way of life, and no tolerance. Sadly, that was my last diverse moment. Amourville smothered my personal expression.

A young woman stepped aboard, clueless, with a sallow child and a baby that hung from her ragged clothes. Pa tugged my shirt, and we offered her our seats. Her child hugged me, and my heart was crushed. Love was not a matter of culture or language or religion. I realized that love was tolerance and generosity. But this would be the last nice gesture since, in Amourville, charity was scarce. The horn honked twice, steam arose from the chimney, and a crew member closed the gate. The port's tumultuous voices evaporated as the ferry sailed away. Soon Port Granada was a memory cluttered with smoke.

The tide shook the ferry like a toy. A deafening silence spread over the deck. My nose cringed from the clash of acrid smoke, and a dry cough overtook me. All passengers focused on a cloud of smoke from the starboard side. Pa and I moved for a closer look. Burnt pieces of metal floated on the water like a puzzle, the cloud of smoke enclosed our boat like a shadow, and everyone began to cough. Red and blue lights rotated on the riverbank, and firefighter boats sprayed water on what seemed like our ferry. Two police boats zipped past our ferry towards the chaos. A sullen murmur rose among the passengers. Pa tried to get a better view of the situation. The captain of our ferry stepped out of the cockpit with his binoculars and frowned. Pa asked me to stay put. The fumes spun my head like a wheel. I covered my ears, but the wails reverberated. Then I shut my eyes, and the darkness took me into a trance…a trance I did not want to wake up from.

Pa shook me several times. My eyes itched, and my throat was irritated. I lifted my head, and the deck was filled with dead silence.

"Are you ok, love?" He asked.

"I am ok. Are we almost there?"

"We are close."

"Why are people sobbing?" I asked. He hugged me.

"Do you remember the ferry we were supposed to take?" I nodded.

"It caught fire and sank, no survivors."

"My friends, the twins too?!" My voice cracked.

"Everyone died… I am sorry, love, that is life…."

I was devastated, but there was another emotion lurking in my mind.......

My friends,   that could have been me
No!   No!   No!   I can't believe in a God that lets
all this pain,   if he is love then he should be nice not mean   I
don't like to pray anymore   pray   pray
pray   and nothing good happens maybe I could die right now
my friends, I will never forget you,
thank you for showing nature   thank you for
being nice   but I don't care what Pa and Ma
say,   I don't like God anymore   he is never nice   always
mean   always wants prayer   but bad things
everywhere......

That was my first experience with death. Then anger arose, the anger of not throwing a tantrum and preventing them from boarding. I wanted to die, be with them, wherever they were. That experience taught me that any moment can be my last, regardless of God's plans--he likely didn't care. If life is fragile, why leave it in anybody's hands?

We arrived at the capital, or the big city as we called it. As soon as the crew opened the gate, everyone swarmed out. We waited for the commotion to settle. I walked to the railing, hoping to see a rescue boat with the twins. Instead, the sky was boundless, the river was calm, and the sun shined over the waters like the last time we played. Their laughter resonated in the wind. Perhaps death was not the end of everything. Perhaps one day we will see each other.

Ma ran to embrace me. Pa stood and tapped my little sister Kashmir on the head. She seemed mad as usual. Then, Ma gave me a gift, a miniature portrait of a girl with a rainbow emerging from her heart. The watercolor was vivid and beautiful. That painting has been a part of my life. It symbolized freedom and happiness, it still does.

Pa hugged Ma, though it seemed a bit forced. Ma was loyal to Pa, even if he mistreated her. But she was always there to wait for him, despite his many travels. I did not want to be like Ma, tied to an absent man who brought her discomfort. I tried to be brave, not tied to anything or anyone like Pa. I preferred to be a man than be loyal to a man or even a woman. Family always came first, and then there was me, only me.

It was a relief to be back home. The mouthwatering smell of beef stew enchants my nostrils. While Ma cooked, I laid in my heavenly bed in my room filled with dolls. I noticed the black doll beside a black boy and the white doll all alone. That moral disorder was probably my sister's or even Ma's idea. I placed two black dolls together kissing, a white doll with a brown boy, a reddish doll with a black boy, and girls with girls, boys with boys. Not everything had to go the way society told me.

The dolls thanked me for taking the shame away and accepting diversity. They jumped into bed and tickled me. The tickles were so intense that tears slipped out the corner of my eyes, and as I looked out my window, we were in the sky, where nobody could see us. My door opened; a giant blue eye shed its tears until it flooded the room. The humming of the waves and the smell of the ocean relaxed me. The twins and Alice laughed, but the water kept rising. My lifeless dolls floated in the water. My screams were futile, and the laughter subsided. Daylight turned to darkness, and a white whirlpool with the full moon in the center sucked out the water through my window. Ominous voices revolved in the vortex, and my skin became wrinkled. When the flood was gone, my body was back on the bed. There was a purpose to these happenings, and it would not be long before I discovered them.

Our tradition was to gather as a family for dinner. Kashmir's eyes were darts that pierced through my skin, and there was an awkward silence except for the clinging of the utensils. Kashmir barely touched her food. Ma looked at both of us while Pa enjoyed his meal.

"Grandma is moving in with us!" We all stared at her.

"Since the passing of Gramps, there is no point in her living in Nicaragua. She will be much happier with us." Pa rolled his eyes, and Kashmir lowered her head.

"I am so happy. When is Grams coming?" I said.

"Possibly next month."

"And you are just telling me this, Sherry?" Pa asked.

"I thought I'd save it for a special family moment like this one."

"I don't like grandma; I don't like nobody!"

Kashmir slammed her utensils and rushed out of the table.

Ma ran after her. Pa stayed at the table as if nothing had happened. He smiled at me and asked me to finish my food. After that, I understood Pa a little more. He loved peace and solitude. He stretched out his hand to caress my head.

"One day, you will make this family proud." He said.

"How, Pa?"

"You must promise to not ever tell anyone, especially your mother." He said.

I nodded… Pa, why did he do that? Why to me? It is best kept a secret…

Pa never trusted anyone, not even Ma. But if Pa loved me, then why was he with Alice? Did he love Alice? I never dared to ask him. I knew people felt love; I knew people had sex, but why did they do all that? Of course, I wanted to make my family and Pa proud, but will I experience love? Will I experience sex? Maybe I was too young to think about that……

why do girls always suffer   why can't they be like boys   maybe we don't need boys   they need us and   really they are just weird, I don't need a boyfriend   then he be like Pa, mean   I do not want to have a period, it sounds so painful, I wish I'd be a boy and kick all boys ass when they are mean!   maybe if I show boys I am strong they will respect me, I'll show the world I am strong, as long as Ma does not know   Pa wanted me to be a boy   then why was I born a girl? God's fault?   Nah!   I am what I want to be   but   but   what was Pa and Alice doing?   Sex? But why? Why do people like it so much?   Oh for kids… then no I don't like kids, I don't want that sex,   but I do need to know,   who really loves me?……

Our little store closed early. The store was Ma's job and Pa's second source of money besides veterinary work. Mother prayed on her knees. Although not unusual of her, I approached her with caution.

"Are you ok, Ma?" She got up,

"Thomas's wife is pregnant! I placed her in my prayers."

My world flipped over. Alice was going to feel the same pain as the mare! She deserved better than just having kids. Unfortunately, it was probably her husband. Poor Alice, I don't pray, but I hoped that she survived. Perhaps the feeling I had at the estate meant we would never see each other again.

Pa drank a beer outside on the veranda. He had a sullen countenance but grinned after each sip. Pa did not seem worried, but those questions lingered in my head. Finally, he asked me to sit next to him.

"How was school?"

"Good. Pa Alice is pregnant. Is she going to die? Is she going to feel pain, like the mare?"

"Maybe, maybe not. Life is unpredictable."

"Pa… what is the point of life?"

He swallowed the last of his beer and looked me in the eyes.

"It goes on, nobody cares about you. Worry about yourself only and you will be happy because you don't know when you will die. So, listen to your Pa…."

A deep conflict developed between what I wanted and what my family thought I should do. Pa's words were too confusing or too profound for me, I don't know. But if that was the point of life, then why live? If any moment could be the last, why worry? I am still confused. But if Pa said it, then he was right; at least, that was my reasoning. I am a result of the little things around me, good and bad. I am not all myself, however, Pa was a refuge, but also, a torture.

Pa hugged me and kissed my forehead. When I looked once more for him, he was gone. It was just reality and I in a meaningless battle. But there was no price too high to pay for owing myself. The price was high, yet I am still here, trying to solve life. Will I ever solve this painful beauty?

2

My grandmother, Pauline Munoz Cruz, or Grams as we call her, puffs a cloud of smoke. It is her custom to smoke a cigar on Saturday mornings. She says the best are Nicaraguan cigars, smooth with hints of chocolate. Good smoke is like therapy for her; she can say the wisest or scariest things, but her words are too abstract sometimes. She likes to call my grandfather, who has been dead for the past ten years. She can even call three times and not remember a thing, which worries me a little. Grams is a brave woman because she beat up my grandfather after he slept with another woman, like a Shakespearean drama. There is a bit of her in me; fearless, independent, and yes, a bitch. Grams tells me her stories, which is why I am telling her mine. Although the wood is decrepit and each step makes an eerie crackle, the veranda is the most peaceful spot in our house. Our garden has sunflowers that dance to the rhythm of the crisp wind. They are like faces, neither happy nor sad… much like me.

Grams shuts her eyes, and a cloud of smoke conceals her face. Twelve years later, the events of the Estrada ranch haunt me; my life is not the same. The past is a broken puzzle, and as the pieces stick together, it reveals why the Rendar family has all these bad blessings. I never believed in the occult nor in God, but there must be an explanation for this calamity and death. Could this be what they call a bad omen? I need answers. I am too young to end my life only because a curse torments me. It is hard to live the life I want. Perhaps society is the greater curse. What will I do with my life? I am done with high school and with alienation. At least with Grams, I can express my thoughts without judgment, without this God, or from the fear of this antique town.

"I cannot interpret your story my dear," Grams says.

"Why not?"

"It is dark and complicated. But it requires a sacrifice, I am pretty sure."

"Sacrifice? So, we are cursed? So, all these happenings are because of a curse?"

"We are cursed. Where is Mikey?" She says.

I roll my eyes. Grams is about to have her strange episodes.

"Who is Mikey, Grams?"

"My friend, he is supposed to be here. Where is he?"

"You don't have any friends, Grams"

"I swear!"

Grams is not all there. I don't blame her; perhaps we were meant to be alone. It's time to take Grams to the psychiatrist. I glance at my watch. Ms. Peggy will fire me for another late arrival. Work and work and work, my only escape. I should start my education. Will I be successful? Or will I stay with Ms. Peggy for the rest of my life? It does not matter anymore. I help her out of the chair, but she yells bloody murder and swings my hand away. She wants to see her friend, but her wails are ear-shattering. The clock ticks, and she does not budge. I am too young for this shit. If only Laura was here, she would be my right hand. But Laura is another incongruence of memory……

> *this old woman will end up ruining what I have left! everything I have done does not mean I deserve this*
> *what have I done?   Some coffee sounds   good right now*
> *I was the oldest, the first one to work, the one to inherit the Rendar fortune,   so why doesn't this lady move!*
> *Laura if you are out there feel me, I know you can*
> *I can't! This is my mother's responsibility!   Poor woman, she laughs on her own   Kelly, Kelly, that is her love I guess,*
> *if we have the same genes   then is this my future   I rather be dead…   so we are cursed fuck but why by who?!*
> *Laura, Laura…   Laura probably hates me now I can't leave my grandmother   but how do I move her!   Coffee, yes coffee   she probably has a caffeine withdrawal   coffee is her drug,   Ma better stop praying in that damn church and come take care of her mother!   The pastor, the imposter more like it   asking me money for a prayer   I hate religion, I need to get out of this town, like now   the coffee……*

The coffee is not on the counter, and I need it for this idea to work. The coffee is likely under the sink. Grams feels Ma and I will steal it. I dump the entire can of coffee in the trash bin. Grams walks into the kitchen, crying.

"It's ok, Grams, join me for coffee, then we can find your friend."

Her eyes sparkle, and she wipes the snot out of her nose. Grams sits patiently for her cup of joe, but I tell her the coffee is gone; there is no sign of coffee in this little kitchen. Then, I shrug, and a loud silence overtakes the kitchen.

"I want to go back to Nicaragua and die there." She whispers.

"Sure, but first, let's go to the big city and get more coffee." I say.

"Yes, coffee sounds good, but what happened to the coffee?"

"We are just... just out, Grams."

"But why do we need more coffee?"

"Don't you want some coffee with Kelly?"

"Who is Kelly?" She looks around.

"Let's get more coffee and then go to Nicaragua." I say.

Grams nods and walks over to get her coat. This plan makes me feel like a wise fool. But, so far, she is buying it.

The central park is the heart of Amourville. Old men gather to play chess and domino, and puffs of smoke permeate the central gazebo–this is where the sick old men scout the repressed young girls. Mr. Phills, the renowned gardener and owner of Phillis Gardening, meticulously mows the park. Any discrepancy would cause an upheaval in city hall. The mayor feels this town is an example of God's order. The essential shops surround the central park. Louis's Groceries and Alan's Convenience Store, Terry's Diner–the most delicious waffles in the world, Jule's Bakery, Lily's Creamery, and Vineyard of Heaven, our only winery, reserved primarily for men, married women, and tourists.

Across from the winery are Carl's Hardware Store and Will's Mechanic Shop. The original founder of the mechanic shop had 20 children, he was really into the church's idea of being fruitful and filling the earth. All the stores are owned by men; their wives and children manage the shops. Good men stay home and read the bible, evil men do things that seem good, but everyone turns a blind eye. Women are under the eye of God; like Eve, they can lead men to do evil. They marry to prevent sin. Next to city hall is the most dreadful place, the church. Everyone's rock, everyone's real illusion, and where faith has a high price, literally.

A newlywed couple steps out of the church, and their guests swarm them with hugs and kisses. This is just what we need, a shameful wedding, to clog the entire streets!

The sad bride clashes eyes with me. She lowers her face and pretends to smile when her husband kisses her. The older men towards the back of the crowd scowl at me. They know what I did and what I stand for, but nobody controls me, not religion, not men. I am what I am. As the traffic dissipates, I step on the gas, and a trail of dust erases their glares. This is Amourville, where marriage is an expectation, love is a taboo, and where everything is either God's blessing or God's curse.

It is a relief to drive one hour to the big city and breathe diversity.

The road to the big city is an endless trail. The rough terrain vibrates the car so much my hands are numb from the tight grip of the wheel. A cloud of dust blinds our path, and my teeth grind from the ghastly creak of metal.

The road hastily joins the main highway, and the dust dissipates and reveals a vast panorama. Vineyards to the right and to my left, fields that produce the best weed. This is known as the valley of escape. The mystical place of the San Joaquin Valley and the most haunted in all of California. Rows of euphoric thoughts grow like flowers into ridges and cast a dreamlike spell that elicits powerful and regretful poetic words. Euphoria, pleasurable and boundless, manipulate every limb and transforms all that is innocent into depravity, like that sneaky night with Laura. In this paradise, anger evaporates, happiness multiplies, and fear of society moves dimly and crumbles into the soil. The farmers plow the hash like shadows swarm up into an impermeable cloud. I do it occasionally, but it brings lots of trouble.

After the valley, a billboard depicts an eye with a halo on top, rays of celestial light emanate from its pupil, and the eye hovers over a golden throne. It reads, *Repent for Jehovah is watching. Join us Sundays for the sermons of Pastor Michael Miller.* That is Ma's place of gossip, the center of oppression for women. My blood curls as we approach it, time moves slower, and its stare bites my skin like a sunburn. Eyes, eyes all over, eyes in my life, always watching me. What does it see? What does it want? Stop looking at me…

I press the gas, but the monstrous billboard remains in sight. This feeling brings me the most regretful flashbacks…

We came to Amourville because Pa was tired of wrestling with forces that stopped every avenue of his success. We were lost in the valley of escape, looking for water. There was a man on the road with a half-dead donkey. Pa pulled over to help him. Pa rehydrated it with our last jug of water, Ma was hysterical, and Kashmir was near a heat stroke. In his great ignorance, the man thought that God had sent us. He led us into Amourville and allowed us to sleep in his home. One day the man returned from church filled with happiness. He gave the house to Pa because Pastor Miller stated it was all a miracle from God. He was old, had no kids, and was a widower. He took off, saying he was going to Jerusalem, and we never saw him again. Pa and Ma became devotees with deep fervor. Pa felt obliged by the town's traditions, and Ma was afraid of this God. Perhaps the eye no longer wants us. The Rendars are cursed. Why does being a grownup have to be so hard? Guilt, freedom…faith, and skepticism. Everything is a choice, but does it really matter if eyes constantly judge you? Nothing good comes from this God.

"The eye, it watches everything but sees nothing." Grams chuckles.

She is right, but it's hard to tell if she is lucid or in her own world. God punishes the innocent or the ones that try to be human. But an eye will not determine my future.

Grams sleeps like a stiff corpse. Vultures circulate in the sky; a dead animal must be near, not unusual for these hot fields. A herd of vultures devours a chunk of carrion. My stomach is a blender, and my jelly legs decelerate the car. The vultures barricade the road. Their eerie stance and hoarse hisses are a sentence to doom. The clock ticks in my head; only one hour left! More vultures join the barricade. One of them jumps on top of the hood and jabs its beak several times into the glass. Grams wakes up and gasps to see these monsters trap our car... she screams bloody murder. I shift into reverse and drift the car back to Amourville. An apocalyptic cloud of vultures' hovers around us. The birds shove the vehicle, and the wheel spins through my hands. Gram's screams pierce through my ears, and their hair-rising wings obstruct the view.

"It is the curse, the curse!" Grams yells.

I pull over to the side of the road. The birds begin to penetrate through the windows.

"Who cursed us, grams?"

"That old woman in the estate put a curse. I can see it!" Her voice muffles...

"What?"

"She cursed the family! She wants you; you must save us!" She says.

The uproarious vultures block my thoughts, but what if these events are really a curse. These vultures cannot be an act of nature. Perhaps I should believe in the supernatural. A carrion-infested beak swirls into a cracked window, and I hold Grams' frozen hands. Laura, my love, forgive me, I love you…is this my end?

Thunder rolls across the valley and spooks the birds; we hold our breath. Lightning bolts illuminate the dark backdrop of clouds. A tinkling sound echoes as the first pearls of rainfall drop onto the roof. Out the window, a torrential wall sweeps across the valley. The drops knock the vultures like punching bags. Finally, the vultures dissipate, and the rain blurs into a long whirring noise. Light shines through the rain. I wipe the fog off the window; there is a welcome sign. *Amourville welcomes you, diversity, friendship, and faith.* The poster depicts a happy family at the bottom, with neatly dressed kids, a mom as a housewife, and a dad as an office worker. A perfect utopia but none of it is true except for the church at a corner. The shining eye is on top of the church. What does it want from me?

The deluge stops, and the sun glorifies the land with its rays. I walk into the middle of the road, and a deafening silence spreads across the valley. Grams breaks the silence with a request to head back home. My shift starts in 30 minutes. Grams takes her pills… she knocks out for the rest of the ride.

A stack of papers stares at me. My wrists tingle, and my eyes burn. This is not what I want to do for the rest of my life, nor do I wish to work at my parents' store. As a straight "A" student, no drama, and no boyfriend; except my sweetheart Joseph, and being a bad bitch, this job can't be my destiny. Data and more data, I can do better than this. Laura is a good teacher. She is no longer here, but it brings me joy to not depend on anyone, not even her. My dream is to be a lawyer, help women and children who can't defend themselves, replace traditions with justice, and replace superstition with reason. Amourville needs to catch up with the world. Pa's pride is to see me as a lawyer. Despite our misfortunes, Pa will always have the most important place in my heart. But with all the creepy things happening to us, it's hard to imagine a future. It is hard to decide whether it's a curse or all in our heads. Perhaps shit just happens……

It hurts, I love you   you love many things that can't love you back,   that is why love is not for me   but Laura,   I need more coffee but   if I get up Ms. Peggy will know I was late   just a cup, ah,   now my stomach growls, maybe Ma did something yummy,   hope Grams is ok I'll   call her during my break if I can get one of   those birds, was that a sign,

a sign of what   curse?   after   everything that maybe there is one   hope it's a bird that pecks the soul and tweets a melody that can't be reached,   if we dare touch it, it flies away, then why hope   I should be a poet, lonely,   hungry   A cardamom cake with coffee Ms. Peggy is in her office, no I have to finish all this before I leave   Williams vs Fermors case#2.22bk14973er, missing documents   Is   she   doing   this   on purpose? my eyes burn, I can't do this anymore   is it the curse?

That woman cursed me, why what did I do?   Perhaps nothing, kids my age want to party and live life, I   I   want people to admire me for my talents, for my contribution to their lives not just sex or traditions or duty   maybe it's a curse, maybe it's a wakeup call   we can aspire to have things that does not mean we

*will get them better to spend life close to the fishes than waste time wishing
I had gills   I want to return to school, but first coffee......*

My office phone rings, and the screen shows Ma's number. The office is dead silent, except for the click-clacks of the keyboards. Ms. Peggy won't hear me. Grams is out of breath. I whisper, but there is no reply. An eerie crack comes out of the speaker. The phone slips out of my hands, and the thud breaks the silence. My eyes scan the office; everything is still serene. Grams pleads for help, static breaks the line… a long dial tone. Ms. Peggy smashes another tower of work on my desk. She looks at me with contempt. It is not worth asking for an early leave. But desperate times call for desperate measures.

Harold Peggy works on his computer. He is diligent, especially when his mother keeps him in check. Harold is obsessed with me; he wants me to sleep with him. But I don't like him, even if he is the last man on earth.

"Harry, I really need your help!" I implore.

He gives me his undivided attention. I sit at the edge of his desk and stroke his head. He looks around and touches my leg.

"I am sorry we have not been able to go out…family issues," I say.

"Oh, but, what… what about now? This is such a s-u-r-p-r-i-s-e."

I stroke his head with tenderness, then push it toward my breasts.

"Can you do me a favor?" He nods.

"I have a family emergency and need to step out."

Harold lifts his head out of my breast and looks at me, dazed.

"Anything for you, princess!"

"But I just don't want your mother to fire me. I want to see you all the time, cutie."

"Under one condition," I guess, even gullible people have conditions. "Promise me you will go on a date with me." He says.

Grams needs me. It is better to lie than to lose a family member. We gently touch lips---this is disgusting---he shuts his eyes, and I keep mine open. He lays back as if he had an orgasm,

"May I go, sweetie, please?" I say.

"Don't worry about mom, I'll excuse you," he grabs me by the arm, "Don't break my heart again." He whispers.

I grin and gently remove his hand from my arm.

A desperate moron like him will never get any girls. Empathy is not one of my qualities, but I'd do anything for my family.

I storm into the living room, but everything seems intact. A ghastly voice travels through the walls. "Ma, Grams!"… No response. The patio lights flicker. Why would they be outside at this hour? Grams sits in our backyard gazebo, illuminated by an array of string lights. She is entertained in the most amicable conversation with that amorphous shadow, the one with a pipe hat. That thing continues to appear all over my house, in my thoughts, and everywhere I go! Why does it stalk me?

Its face is unidentifiable, and those two red eyes tense my entire body. Grams enjoys the company, but Ma needs to see this. I take a picture of it with my phone. Where the hell is Ma? In the kitchen, a large butcher knife lies on the table. "Mother!"…Still no response. There is a small trail of blood that leads to Pa and Ma's bedroom. "Sherry!" Grams yells from the garden. I rush to help her.

Grams walks towards me. The shadow is gone, but no signs of Ma.

"Grandmother, what is going on? Where is Ma?"

She drops herself into my arms without an answer. She then heads back inside. The string lights go out, and the crickets chitter. My feet trip over a pile of dirt. It seems to be a hole or something. A sudden pang stiffens my body and cuts my breath. No words can describe this; everything turns dark…

The sun's rays penetrate through the gazebo's cracked roof, and my eyes squint from the itching heat. The garden spins a little, and my back aches. But no pain is strong enough to erase last night's visions… Grams!

Grams enjoys a cup of coffee at the kitchen table. She pours me a cup aloof and in peace.

"Who was that thing you spoke with last night?"

"What thing, my dear?"

I pull out my phone and search for the photo… the shadow is no longer on frame. I change the brightness, lower the contrast, and play around with the exposure but nothing. I pull the coffee away from Grams.

"Grandmother, is this part of the curse?" She shrugs.

Each glance at the photo forces me to question reality… Is this all real or an illusion of my mind? Do curses exist?

Grams watches a soap opera in the living room. Yet, she remains calm without medication. The shadow people need to leave; I want my life back. I am tired of this crap!

Light catches the corner of my eye. The shine comes from Pa's drawer. These supernatural episodes just get weirder and weirder. My stomach swirls and a force grabs my hand and pushes me to open the drawer. This cannot be a nightmare because nightmares are absurd. There is a clear purpose to opening this drawer.

The drawer has some of my Pa's odds and ends, but an old photograph traps my attention. It is the group photo we took outside the Estrada estate. But Pa's head is missing, and so is mine. Thomas and Alice have sullen expressions, and that old woman stares like an owl at night. My hairs rise at the echo of her voice. There is a peal of sinister laughter in the room. I look around, but there is nobody here. Her evil chant!

"Get out of here! Leave me alone!" I yell, but the chant continues through the ambiance.

My sight turns to a vignette, and a black hole with purple lightning bolts surrounds the house. Strings of light emerge from the floor, my skin sparkles, and a wrinkled hand arises out of the photo and reaches for my heart. I try to pull away, but my neck is a stone, the hand's claws rip a piece of my skin…Rose!

Grams stands in the doorway with a sorrowful smile. The room is dead silent, and the old photo is intact.

"Now, do you believe?" Grams says.

I drop the photo and embrace Grams with a hug. That evil witch is the reason my family suffers. I don't know why she cursed me, but I must break the curse. Otherwise, my family will be cursed forever. We must face things that life throws at us, even if we don't like those things. That is part of growing up.

An anvil falls on my chest, my throat tightens into a knot, and I rush out to the veranda for fresh air. What if everything right now is a confusion, a joke? What if pain was really pleasure? Perhaps not, the pain my family endures is not a joke. The pain is real, disguised as blessings. They are bad blessings.

It hurts me to think of an uncertain future, yet I must believe in the unreal, in the things that I don't know, the things that I can't see. I must have faith that this is a story. If this is a story, my actions will ensure a good ending. All stories end, some in death, some in happiness. Perhaps this one will end somewhere in the middle. If this is not a story, then all of this is an illusion of my mind, shadows in a cave, or perhaps the world is more messed up than we think. But if the happenings are in my head, it must all be a story. I don't know anymore.

"Don't look for meaning in the noise of words. Instead, listen to the silence." Grams says.

Perhaps there is hope. Perhaps God has some answer, even if it is hard to trust in him. But no... I am going to solve the problems of life. It is absurd to avoid facing my reality, my search for answers. My existence matters: it must be the answer to life. The meaning of my life? The purpose of the Rendars? We will see…

The highway is long, but the destination is inevitable. The road covers me in rocks and glory. I proceed like Jehovah, who never cries, and like Satan, who never prays. My mind is the tree whose strength needs water yet never implores it. I will break the curse of the Rendar family. Forgive me, my dear love, you are all I have left in this world, but I will ensure you have a good life, free of the curse.

3

It is as clear as the heavens above my head that my life is a shapeless mass of sh… oh no, oh no…no bad words, God will punish me! My years rush like a train, getting too old, but God is good. I must work for my husband and family. Rose and Kashmir, the light of my eyes, so glad they are not like me, beautiful like their mother, yes, but not like me tied to this good-for-nothing husband. Ah, Rose, feisty and stubborn. If I had that attitude, Ruben would be dead by now. Oh! *¡La Sangre de Cristo!* The holy blood of Christ! Forgive me! I need to read the big book a lot more. I really should not say that in church. Pastor Miller will suspend me, Jenny might not talk to me, and Mrs. Wordsworth—what a dream to get up in the morning, sip good coffee, and write poetry. Poetry is the best way to ignore life; I envy her. I shouldn't, but as Mrs. Wordsworth tells me… I am just a clerk. She is right. I am just a clerk.

Sister Wordsworth's husband is the mayor. He cheats on her with a younger woman, but our church turns a blind eye. Perhaps my life is a little better, I think…no, not really. If only someone could listen to me. At least the town reads her poems in the *Rambler*—our local newspaper. Nobody listens to me. God, please send an angel to tell me that it's my duty to care for mom, to love such a loveless husband, and raise unruly daughters. My hunger for whom I could have been eats me from inside. But God keeps me here.

Ruben is bitter nowadays, although he returns happy after his errands in Solvang. He is my bad blessing because he sustains me but now has me trapped like a bird in this store. The store bores me but keeps me alive. It is better than just cooking and cleaning all day.

¡Dios mio! My God! I am tired of that too! I am tired of life… but his tall stature, wavy black hair, and muscular complexion, my Ruben, but now you are an ogre. I am not tired of dreaming. To dream is to sleep awake and forget about reality, just for a little bit, even if reality hurts. If only I can be like Rose, but it does not matter now. Without me, hell would break loose in this house. My family needs me; that is my duty.

My eyes glance around the store. Bottles missing in the fridge, storage boxes neatly stacked in the corners, stale produce scattered in the racks, and medicine; the cure at my fingertips, yet nothing cures me. I keep the rows in order or try to, but my joints hurt a lot. But the floor is shiny, and the ambiance has the fresh smell of disinfectant. Perhaps we must paint these dull beige walls and switch the flickering lights. The store is cramped and cold but essential to the neighborhood. Ruben still sells animal medicine; maybe those can cure me.

The morning crowd is the best. Parents come in for milk and eggs, those working in the big city come for their packed lunches and coffee, and the old folks come to chat about Europe, Los Angeles, Yosemite, and Carmel. Those conversations are as close as I will get to adventure. Amourville is my burial ground. The same faces, sometimes new faces, and sometimes some faces die.

Something is wrong with me. An illness without any symptoms. Cunning and strange, it hides in my entrails and then jumps in the narrow-assorted rows of the store. But when I can't find the illness, I tell myself there is nothing wrong, that life is right. But then, Billy, my old customer, walks in.

"My Sherry, you like espresso?" He asks the same question every day.

"I love it!"

"When you make some?"

He places two cardamon cakes and a cup of coffee on the counter.

"Ay, don't know, maybe tomorrow. They take too much work."

"You come with me."

"Then who working here…."

"Ay, not for me, Harry Sanchez is in town, he very sick, ay, he might die, poor guy."

"What? He moved out of state long ago, he, ok? Harry?"

"I thinking… he says is bacteria, they say is pneumonia, you know pneumonia…."

"*¡La Sangre de Cristo!* Pneumonia, his life is in danger, you sure?"

"Not so so sure, but you go, see him."

Harry, my Harry,   you be dead now, oh my Lord Jehovah forgive me for wishing death, and for adultery in my heart   there he goes again with his motorcycle accident,   I am glad he is alive but still   annoying!   Did   he pay?   Yeah… um yeah he paid, ¡La Sangre de Cristo! what will Ruben want for dinner… GALLO PINTO-- rice and beans   uy!, soup, it is cold   hahaha need to work here, close here then go be good housewife   but   Harry, why would he come back to town   I was the only person that tied him to here   not me anymore,   I am a married woman is he looking for me   he loved me, he promised me that we would leave far from here ay! ay! ay!   it is there, just by his name…Harry…   what is this,   it burns in my chest my heart? I still like Harry,   he was my first kiss, my first love   after all these years he comes to save me!   Is that Ruben?   No, no   too much nervous but he has nothing here, where is he? I should go see him, oh if only I live another life, how happy, maybe   maybe   maybe   love will give me one last chance……

Billy's anecdotes are a play of fact and fiction. Sometimes, I cannot tell the difference. For once, he brings me a novelty. Harry's presence intrigues me, but no! This is a test from the devil. God's commandments are in me. Marriage is sacred to God. I am nobody without Ruben. Ruben is the only person I can count on sometimes.

"Ay, where he at?" I say.

Billy prepares to leave.

"Aya think, um, a lady named Yaritza, living by the valley."

"His cousin, I remember."

"You got to go!"

"I'll ask Ruben. Have a good day."

The store closes in 15 minutes. Ruben enters to do an inventory check and count the register. The sunsets and the crisp wind chills all my bones. There is a scary whisper in the air, *Harry… Harry…* What is that? The wind blows the autumn leaves through the street, a man stands in the whirlwind, he looks strangely familiar… Harry, is that you? The wind blows the silhouette.

"You ok? Close up already!" Ruben shouts from the counter.

The wind subsides, and the street is soulless. As a Christian woman, I should see a dying man because his death will consume whatever is left of me. I must go; Pastor Miller says faith means to honor truth above our friends. The truth is that I wish to be a good Samaritan. But also, for love.

My fingers mangle in the door frame. I grit my teeth to hold my scream. Ruben is too busy counting money… Can't hold it… Ahhh!

Ruben smashes his hands on the counter. He grabs my hand and pours cold water from the bottles in the nearby refrigerator. He then ties a white cloth around my fingers. Then, with a throbbing hand and squirmed nerves, I sweep as usual.

"What are you doing, Sherry?" He says.

I look at him with the most distressed expression. Such is my life.

"Go to the house and prepare dinner. Sweep this later."

"What do you want for dinner?"

"Shrimp and avocados, not too spicy, not too bland."

"Yes…" I sweep the remaining dust.

"Now, Sherry! Your mother needs you, and the girls will come soon!"

Mother spills some coffee on the cracked white counter. That is all she eats, coffee and cardamom cakes, rice with beans. After all these years, it doesn't bother me to clean up after her, I am a daughter before a wife. Harry pops into my head. Lord, help me; these urges are hard to resist. I am a housewife and a mother; protect me. Rose walks into the kitchen with glossy eyes.

"What is wrong, mama?" I say.

"I am ok, Ma." Her voice cracks.

I hope she quits her job and decides to go to college. Rose swallows a full glass of rum. Saliva drowns my insignificant response because she listens to nobody but her father. Then, she serves herself another glass.

"Stop, love." I mumble.

She scowls; that demonic glare is just like Ruben's. Smoke permeates the kitchen. Ruben will be furious, especially after he sees Rose drunk—I would not put it past him to join her.

"Rose dear, I have to tell you something." I say.

"Let me guess…Pa is treating you bad…."

"No, it's about someone, you see, I…." She cuts me off.

"Ma, stop with the soap operas!"

"I do not watch those. That is a sin."

"It is a sin to destroy yourself for someone. I don't want to hear you complain about Pa."

THE BAD BLESSINGS

What can this 19-year-old tell me about sin? Drunk, disrespectful, and independent. Envy stirs inside me, it shouldn't, but it does. No amount of pain or pleasure moves her, lifeless little girl yet free as a bird.

"Anyhow, Ma, can you shave one side of my hair tomorrow?" She says.

As if my work weren't enough. Rose is nice when she is up to something.

"Sure, love..." I say.

Perhaps she might listen to my desire to see Harry. Desire? What am I saying? It is faith that leads me, faith in what... love? Love your neighbor... but I think I love him...

Rose insists I shave her hair by tomorrow. Harry might not have that much time....... *Harry,   how do you look like now those almond blue eyes,   that neat mustache,   your ebony hair   you must still be young   just as I left you   Ruben is going to kill me what to do?   Rice and beans!   Shave the side of her head,   loca! She will look like a boy,   she is such a machona too tomboy   shrimp and avocados are ruined   ay! ay! ay!   Ruben will beat me   Ruben you monster,   can't stay awake, need some rest   has mom eaten? She needs her coffee,   no she needs to eat a bit, Harry there you are! What are you doing   get out of here!   I am a happily married woman, live your own life!   Why can't I do as I please… just fuck everything and be like Rose! ¡Ay! ¡Dios mio!   Stop   Stop……*

Peace with my past is the only way to save my sanity. Ruben steps into the kitchen and cringes his nose. He gives Rose a kiss on her forehead.

"Sorry dear, I was speaking with Rose. I am making rice and beans." My voice trembles.

He sneers and sits with Rose. One day they will regret everything and see the true Sherry. Kashmir walks into the kitchen. Ruben can't stand her; he never did.

"Let me help you, mother!" As Kashmir kisses my forehead.

"Thank you, my love." I say.

Kashmir gives Ruben the warmest greeting. Ruben ignores her.

"We are having an important conversation here," Rose says.

"Oh, not again." Kashmir replies.

"Again, what?!" Rose makes an aggressive gesture. Ruben swallows his glass of rum.

"Stop it, both of you! Kashmir, please help me finish dinner." I say.

Ruben is the instigator, his love for Rose is unreasonable. I am tired of this scenario, but this is my life. I need a new one.

The rice and beans are ready, thanks to Kashmir. Ruben beats me if I ruin dinner.

"It's ok Ma. Rose was born to be a bitch." Kashmir whispers.

We all sit at the table for dinner. Mother joins us. Ruben prays, and then there is an awkward silence. The only sound comes from the clinging of the utensils.

"Ma, can you please make your signature dish. I want to invite Michael over for dinner." Kashmir says.

"Sure, love, but when is he coming?"

"Friday night."

"Lord, that is only two days from now, your father and I will have to switch shifts at the store."

"I can't. I have plans." Ruben says.

"Ma please, you have to do it. He is the love of my life. We will marry soon."

Mother widens her eyes. My mouth drops, but Ruben is indifferent. This is all a sign from God. It is best to let go of the past and focus on the here and now.

"Ma, I need you to say yes!" Kashmir says.

Ruben tosses his utensils and gets up from the table. Rose follows him.

Who says yes to me? I am constantly ridiculed. Stupid little girl, what does she know about love. I am the one that needs to see Harry. For once, I must say no to others and yes to myself.

"Sure, my dear, I'll help you." God help me...

Ruben tosses himself into bed. He still cannot break that old habit of watching tv late at night. He breaks my sleep.......

¡Dios mio!   no matter how much I say it, nothing...   maybe I should not do this   Harry,   how could you catch pneumonia? Poor man, parents die when he was young,   no siblings,   no house,   only a strange cousin and now an illness   not a lover   maybe I   was   his   only   a handsome man like him?   I am sure he had many   but then why is he here!   My   intentions   are   Christian, not evil   ay! but now I have to shave Rose's hair,   cook for Kashmir's boyfriend......

Ruben tilts towards me. His breath smells horrible, as it has been for years.

"Take over my shift tomorrow. I don't feel too well." He blabbers.

"But Ruben, I must help the girls and take my mother to the doctor." I say.

He grabs the pillow and smacks me. My love and respect are gone.......

How could he, son of a bitch!   God do not condone this, I am faithful to you please protect the weak   Give me strength to endure this demon!   Harry, my love, save me, If I get to see you, we are running away like we planned 19 years ago   Pneumonia, how do you kill pneumonia   injection? Pills? Ay!   I can ask the doctor, and maybe   I   can save his life.......

It is a slow day at the store, typical for a Thursday, especially after Wednesday night service at church. This shift is unfair. Ruben should do the inventory. The phone rings. It is my mom's doctor. It pains me, but we cannot attend the appointment. I dare ask:

"What is the cure for pneumonia?"

"With antibiotics, mam, why is she ok?" The nurse asks.

"She has some cough and chest pain."

"Then take her to an ER quickly!"

"She is ok. But what kind of medicine cures pneumonia?"

"Antibiotics, please get her to a hospital!"

"I will. Is it pills or injections?"

"Any will do…."

What a dreadful conversation. Thank God my mother is not sick. But this means my dear Harry needs antibiotics now. Mother screams for coffee.

"Mother, we are leaving in a bit." I say.

Rocks roll inside my head. My mother still has diazepam in her cabinet. Diazepam will knock her out and allow me to think. She swallows them without water and yells bloody murder.

Ruben's bovine medicine is nearby, filled with syringes and pill bottles. They are antibiotics…this seems to be my only hope to save Harry and do something great for once in my miserable life. I call Ruben.

"Dear, a customer is asking if animal antibiotic works on humans."

"What? Who asks?"

"Billy, his brother is sick. I don't want to give him wrong information."

"The injections maybe, not sure. Don't sell them. They must see me before. And stop bothering me." He hangs up.

THE BAD BLESSINGS

Finally, my mother is deep asleep. This is my only chance to save Harry. Even if Harry was my enemy, we learned to love our enemies in church. In all honesty, I am still in love with him.

We arrive at Yaritza's house. This old cottage is full of bittersweet memories. Ruben thinks we are at my mother's appointment. He does not care, which is an advantage right now. Mother is next to me, still asleep. But if we take too long, Ruben will be furious. Not all good things last forever.

The wind blows the leaves off the stony walkway. The cottage is dilapidated, covered in vines and sorrow. The dirty blinds are closed, and the cracked front door has faded red color. Each step tightens my throat. The big book says that for those who help others, the Lord will help them. *Ay, Dios,* please help me. Knock, knock, my arms shiver… still no answer. This is the burial place of my heart. An old woman with glistening blue eyes and frizzy white hair opens the door.

"Sherry, is that you?" She says in a somber tone.

"Hello, Yaritza…" I say.

"I have heard your name all my life. Perhaps today will be the last." She says.

"I just came to see Harry, Yaritza."

She simpers and invites me in. People change, except for Yaritza. She never married, she never found love…

The cottage is dark and dead silent, except for the crackling of the dim fire by the chimney. The stench of mold tickles my nose, and rods of light scatter in my eyes. Yaritza gently opens a door, and a window glare shines on her cadaver-like countenance. I put a mask on since it might be contagious. I should have this love, but it is absurd to want something that does not exist. What if it still exists? Will my life change? There is no turning back now…

Harry lies on a wooden cot, frail and defeated. He shivers from a fever; I shiver from excitement. Yaritza hands me an old stool and shuts the door. He opens his eyes, and his smile is a beam of light that illuminates my life and the dark room.

"You should not be here." He gasps.

"Billy told me. I came to help you."

"I wrote to you, the war was over, but you married." He says.

"I was 18, my father was a monster, my family poor. What was I supposed to do?"

"Leave Sherry. Our love died a long time ago. I'll be gone soon."

"I came to cure you. This injection will cure your pneumonia."

"Do you love me?" He coughs. My heart beats faster. We look into each other's eyes for a long silent moment.

"You still don't stand up for what you feel. You have not changed...." He says.......

He read my mind!   ¡Dios mio!   Only your true love can do that   but I can't say it, It can't but he is right   I love him!   But I am afraid   afraid   Hopefully mom does not wake up screaming......

"Let me die. I don't want to live in pain." He says.

Tears fill my eyes. I hold his hand.

"Let me die in peace, and I will forgive you in this life and in paradise." His voice cracks.

He cannot die. Even if it's not with me, he deserves happiness. My purpose is to save him, but time is almost up. I fumble with my purse and pull out the syringe. Ruben says it might work, but if it kills him, then...God knows my heart.

"This will put you to sleep. You will no longer feel pain." I whisper.

Harry grabs my sweaty wrist. He makes this decision harder and harder. Should I give him what he wants? Or should I do what my heart feels is right? I don't think God can help me here.

"I trust you...." He cringes on his teeth.

I plunge the needle into this leg. His grip gradually weakens, and then his eyes shut. But Harry's heart still beats...

"Thank you, my love…." He gasps.

Is he alive? Or is he dead? I can't stay here to watch. If he survives, then he will thank me one day. If he dies… I don't know. I don't want to know. Finally, I kiss his hand and leave the room.

"He will be fine." I tell Yaritza.

She smirks and escorts me out of the house. It feels good to do this. It must be the right decision. Ay, those purple chrysanths. There is my young Harry promising me endless love… I guess we did keep our promise.

Sundays are my days off. After church, I nap to gain enough energy for the week. But it is common for Ruben to call me to take over his shift. It's always the same excuse, errands to the big city. Could he be seeing someone else? At his age? Nobody likes him, not even the customers. My duty, however, is to care for my family. Kashmir usually helps me cook, but it is strange not to see her this time. It's 3:10pm, and with no sign of Ruben, I rush to the store.

Ruben digs his hands into my frail hair.

"Where is the antibiotic!" Ruben yells.

Billy stands by the counter, and Ruben asks me again with a tighter grip.

"I don't know. A customer needed it for a horse!" I say.

THE BAD BLESSINGS

Billy leaves. Ruben slaps me, swings my head, and finishes me with a punch. My cheek burns, the roots of my hair itch, and the store blurs. Rose helps me up, and she stops Ruben's final strike. Then, behind her shoulder, the most unexpected sight occurs.

Harry steps into the store, vigorous and tall. We all exchange glances as the deafening silence builds tension. Finally, I gather the courage to look him in the eye. Ruben prepares to strike him, but Rose stops his hands.......

¡La Sangre de Cristo! He is alive! I did the right thing, I am a righteous Christian woman, God will allow me into paradise,   I saved my love from death   and there is no greater sign of love than feeling pain for the things that we love,   like Christ   I will be whipped for my love   for my passion   for the only person that makes me happy......

"You lied, Sherry; you saved my life," Harry says.

I go on my knees. God…send an angel to appease this situation. Don't stand for violence; vindicate my rights.

"I must live with the pain of seeing you suffer next to this monster. Now you will get the love you worked so hard for." Harry's voice cracks.

I bow my head. Harry wipes his eyes and leaves. Ruben stares at me for a moment. My back cringes in anticipation of the strike but he storms out the back door.

This is the last time we will see each other. When Harry turns back, he never returns. At least that's the Harry I remember. Harry loves me. He knows I want the best for him. My true love is not dead. I am in his heart wherever he goes, although he might not think of me. Maybe just maybe… one day, not too far, when things change in Amourville, I will see him again. But that's just imagination. Rose helps me up, and I whimper on her shoulder.

This is not God's punishment. It was the right thing to do. Imagination is not about things that don't exist. It is simply to want the best, even if reality strikes us. I need to take care of myself, somehow, someday. Mother's medication is on the counter. God, she needs it now. I'll take a few just to get that feeling. The self is all I will take when I die…….

I am in the sky, this is peaceful   I can fly, my body is like a feather   sins, problems, life, family, love   it is all gone   I am powerful, I am beautiful   I love it   ay! ay! ay!   The clouds,   a nap in the clouds sure looks good   This is life I want to live here, and   if   by the time   I wake up the world is still real and shitty,   I'll ask never to be awakened again……

4

Fuck it! Fuck it all! I need to get away. After my grand adventures, I neglect the quality of my experiences. Sex, love, pleasure, work, food, money, and family, but is this way of life even good for me? Old age is upon me, and I am proud of all my whims and wishes, except for one… writing. Sherry, the store, and this house's strange happenings consume me. I know what a good life looks like from the outside. But how does a good life feel from the inside, where I can truly experience all my life's work. I want to suck the last drops of nectar from my life, but something holds me from the throat. What holds me back? I don't know. Life is a big problem. What is the solution? Love…I don't get much of it, though, Sherry? Well, she is good at cooking and cleaning, but she is frigid and ignorant as a mare. She is no good. It's over; my body hurts. If there is life after death, who cares? A good life is one where death is welcomed without any regrets.

I wake up and thank life for its absurdity. Then there is the same routine. The family portraits strewn around the cracked yellow walls constantly remind me of my accomplished failures. The piano next to the coffin-like door, my little Rose dances to Chopin. My dusty bookshelf is next to Sherry's desk, where she reads the big book and hopes for a miracle. Vines cover the walls like spider legs. The stench of wet dirt permeates the room, irritates my nose, and tiny dots of mold gather around the wall. A small space with massive memories. Alone with my cup of coffee, these words haunt me: what do I do now?

Pleasure exhausts me. The time has come to leave my old life behind and live independently. Amourville is a shit hole, the worst place on earth to die. But the forest is paradise on earth. The perfect place to find the meaning of life. My Rose, the light of my eyes, my heart will rip to not see her. Rose must have the Rendar inheritance. My last duty is to ensure she and my grandchildren are set for life. Sherry is dumb. I don't love her, and Sarah needs a younger man. Sex is great, but things get old. Women, sex, and love, it's over for me. A breakup serves Sarah well.

The church does not have a penny from me. My savings went into the perfection of my cabin in the forest, free of God's mercy. Rose will oversee my retirement funds. She is the only thing that brings me joy. Even when I die, she will be with me in paradise. Humans disgust me, but loneliness is better. Wisdom arises in loneliness. In loneliness, I will be a philosopher. All I want is a quiet secluded life, with little material things, away from society, absorbed in nature, and to write about the essential facts of life. My extraordinary life must inspire others. My wisdom will improve the world, maybe not too much, but just a tiny improvement.

My boys should arrive for poker. Better get the beers out on the veranda. Outside we are safe from Pauline's shouts. Hopefully, that old fart dies soon.

Dillon, Eric, and Eithan arrive with cases of beer. Czech pilsner and IPAs. We take our usual seats and begin a game of poker. Our high school friendship will sadly come to an end.

"Since Britney left, I took it hard and fell off the cart." Dillon says.

"My only true love was Jessica, half French half Korean. I think of her everyday… everyday." Eric says.

"Morons, has life taught you nothing? Men and women are not meant to be monogamous!" Eithan chuckles as he sips his pilsner. Dillon opens an IPA, 12%, and we all stare at him.

"The best way to get rid of sorrow is to drown it…." Dillon says.

"Carmen and I still have a great relationship. No strings, just sex and whiskey." Eithan lifts his bottle.

He pulls out a fancy pocket dagger. "This little guy was a gift from her. It has saved me in the toughest moments." He kisses it, "I will have it on the table for good luck, boys."

"And you, great veterinarian? Local businessman?" Eric asks……

That is what I was   my hand looks good, I am going to win   life is like a game of cards, you don't show your hand, you don't show your move Dillon is getting drunk, old men and alcohol don't mix   the peanuts with salt and lime are good   it's time to tell them about my plans, but it's going to be sad,   is that Rose?   I wonder what they have, maybe a bet no I don't want to owe anything,   I want to go to live in the woods already   why is this so hard?! Can't they just play   wow, this beer is strong   the veranda spins a little   I am going to miss these good times why would a customer need antibiotic?   They usually call me for that, oh well Sherry can handle it   I am fully retired from life......

They all stare at me, waiting for my complaints.

"Any lady troubles?" Eithan says.

"Sex gets old, love does not exist, and life sucks." I say.

"You have everything a man wants," Dillon says

"But not the way I want it...."

A somber silence overcomes the game, then we put our cards on the table. Eithan gets three of a kind, Eric a full house, and I get nothing. Finally, Dillon stares at his hand and places his cards on the table, royal flush 10 JQKA.

"Even without Britney, alcohol is still at my side." Dillon laughs, and we pat him on the back.

"Well, I think my life is over." They all stare at me again.

THE BAD BLESSINGS

"I can't even play right!"

I grab Eithan's dagger and motion a jab against my chest.

We all tremble by a sudden roll of thunder, the sky turns gray, and droplets clatter on the roof. The droplets turn into a downpour. All my friends disappear except Dillon, who stares at me. Rays of light come out of his head, and he points to the rain.

Is that me and my father? The rain does not touch them, but they are there, glowing. Father beats me, like in my young days. "Be a man!" My father's voice echoes in my head. Don't hit me, father, please don't hit me! The vision evaporates. Thelma appears in the rain, naked like the night she popped my cherry. Prostitutes are great… she was the best, my first love. But Thelma's thin complexion turns into a pool of blood. Her blood smears all over my clothes. Dillon vanishes into thin air, and my father's laughter echoes away.

Eric appears shrouded in a black robe that leaves nothing visible but his face and bony hands that point to the rain. Kashmir bleeds on the floor, almost disfigured. Sherry and Pauline strangle each other. Rose's belly protrudes and explodes. An angel with a sword emerges from Rose's guts, and his luminance blinds me. The vision turns to fumes like the previous one.

Eithan replaces Eric. Eithan turns into a ghoul with pale wrinkled skin, sunken black eyes, and hideous hairy wings.

He points to the rain. I hide his dagger in my pocket. I can see my cabin, cozy and blissful, but I run through the woods naked. Wings sprout from my back, and a beautiful angel joins me. It looks like a female. Her face is blurry but strangely familiar. She pulls out a saber and rips my guts out. Blood covers the veranda, and I shut my eyes. Is this the end?...

My eyes blink, the rain dissuades, the sun peeks through the clouds, and my three buddies sit with their beers......

What the hell was all that! I maybe drank too much, or I need sleep   more coffee, coffee always helps   ok, they need to leave, these morons are just too much   I hate my life, I hate my stupid family   and I just hate them!   I got to leave to the woods   those visions were a wake-up call   to leave   leave they might come true   and I can't bare it, yes everything happens for a reason......

Eric waves his hand in front of my eyes.

"Guys, what was that rain all about?" I say.

They all exchange glances.

"I am serious...." I assert.

They place their cards on the table.

"Ruben, you have just been staring into the distance, are you ok?" Eithan asks.

THE BAD BLESSINGS

The time has come to break away from the things that no longer matter.

"I must make a declaration. This is our last game. I am leaving for my cabin in the woods…forever." They all gasp.

"My life flashed before my eyes, and now it is time for me to go." I say.

A somber silence overcomes them.

"I will always love you guys, but you can always visit me…once…in a while…." I mutter.

Eric puts the cards away. Eithan pulls out a bottle of rum from his jacket.

"Well, let's make a toast then…." Eithan says. We hold up our shot glasses. "To our everlasting friendship!" The alcohol trickles down my throat, and the world spins a little more.

"Ruben, how are you going to leave Sarah? She is not going to let you go that easily." Eithan says.

"Sarah!" We shush Eric.

"Sherry does not know, wise guy." Dillon says.

"Yeah, her, well…." I say.

"No more lead in your pencil?" Eric says, they all laugh.

"No, you morons! I will break up with her, simple as that."

"Maybe you can get that sack of bones… what's his name? The one that signs documents." Eric says.

"Um… Henry Miles, the notary?" I say.

"Yes! He falsifies papers. Maybe he makes a fake document, and you show it to Sarah."

Eithan smacks Eric in the back of his head. Eric turns around, dumbfounded. We all crack up.

"Well then, let's have another toast!" Eithan pours another round of rum. "To a peaceful breakup and a great friendship!" We take the shot. We all burst into laughter.

"We are still buddies, right, Ruben?" Eric asks. I really don't want to see them again.

"Yes…of course, my friends…." I reply. They all pat my back, and we finish our round of beer.

My head is a blender. Their laughter resonates in my head, and my vision is blurry. Nothing stands in the way of my goals, not even Sarah. The door, where is the door? Game over. My body crashes into the bed; everything is dark. That rum is good, my, I make too many errors, goals, goals, they are cool but no more friends, my head…

I can no longer find things in my old store, and my head explodes. An antibiotic is missing! Finally, some Alka-Seltzer with water, the bitter bubbles cringe my mouth. I lay my head back on the chair…who would buy an antibiotic without consulting me? The stack of receipts shows no trace of an antibiotic sale. Dumb Sherry giving credit again. Soon, I won't deal with her anymore. Billy walks into the store. I will miss Pauline more than this creature, but he does not have any animals. Sherry storms into the store......

> *Sherry deceived me!   After all, I have sacrificed for her!*
> *Bitch is a bitch! Sherry with a lover, clever move,   I   am such a moron!   67   years   of   life   to   be   cheated   like   this   I need a drink   or a smoke   Rose   is coming,   a bimbo like Sherry would never...   oh crap she does not care of the goals of a real man   it is all my fault and now I will fix it   The right thing to do, let go of shit......*

Sarah's porcelain face glistens as she opens her door. The stench of burning food cringes my nose. Portraits hang all over her studio. The wooden floor squeaks as I take one last glance at these surreal paintings. A man with a bloody heart and deep purple background; hues of red, orange, pink, and yellow. I never knew its meaning, but she says it symbolizes life. A beautiful woman kisses a shapeless man, she says it is love, I can't understand it. A wall of grilles separates her painting studio and kitchen. Sarah is 30 years old; she is a talented artist with a promising career. She comes from wealth and does not need anything from anyone. Her tragic flaw... men, or at this moment, me. She always finds a way to please me, but I am tired of her.

Sarah attempts to cook. Her long golden hair and stunning white dress do not belong near the kitchen. She serves me a glass of cognac and sits on my lap.

"Why haven't you visited me?" She caresses my neck.

"I have a family and a business." I say.

The sweet cognac burns my saliva. Sarah rolls her eyes. She then serves me a bowl of soup.

"I made it, especially for you, sweetheart…."

The smell is unbearable, the soup too thick, and the broccoli dissolves like mush.

"It is delicious…." I wipe my mouth and serve myself another glass of cognac.

"Finish the soup now!" Sarah demands.

"I am not hungry."

I toss myself on a red chaise sofa. Sarah rips her dress off. Naked, she rubs her ass on me and unbuttons my shirt. She moves down and looks at me with her emerald eyes. One last time the tiger feeds on the prey……

Is it going? It seems as if it is going?   I   feel   it   but Come on This feels great, but I don't think it is going to work, oh yeah, that is amazing   but   why   is   it   not working…… She does it like a goddess.   I tackle Sarah one last time.

she gasps and laughs in the same breath. Harder and harder… I can't anymore, I must slow down… she slows her spasmodic movements and presses her angelic hands on my chest, and pushes herself inside me, but it is over……

"Sarah, it is over." I say.

She scowls and steps away from me.

"It has been a great adventure, but now I want to be alone." I say.

Sarah moves to the kitchen. She returns with a full glass of champagne and slams the bottle on a nearby table.

"Alone or another woman, or Sherry?" Her voice cracks.

"Alone…"

"Cowshit! Who is going to want you, a weak old man." She chugs the entire glass.

"Have you been drinking?"

She serves another glass and downs it in one gulp.

Sarah is young and beautiful, and she can find a young man anywhere. I don't care about her. Now is the time for her to learn that love does not exist. Love only exists in her paintings; that is all.

"Sarah, I loved you, but I love myself more. I came to break up. You know we have been going down a rocky road for the past year. The time has come to finish this."

I put my clothes back on. She swallows another glass and serves herself again.

There is no remorse in this decision because Rose will hate me if she discovers this affair. Feminism is another of her flaws. Sarah goes to the floor to cry. Will she kiss my morning breath? Will I last in bed? Will she deal with my ailments? Will she cheat on me with a young man who can have kids? In the end, will we be able to sit down and speak about life and living? Death and purpose? No…This is the right thing to do. This could have gone worse, but she can drown in her pain. Sarah knows how to care for herself.

Sarah is drunk and full of rage. She throws the champagne bottle on the floor and makes a thunderous mess. Then, before my hand reaches the doorknob, Sarah pulls me by the shirt.

"You either stay, or your little Rose will know who her father really is!" She complicates things with the most dreadful words.

"Please don't do that. Don't even go there…." I whisper.

"To keep you, I would do anything, even destroy what you love."

I would also do anything to keep Rose's love. She wins the battle, but I am not giving up.

"Fine, do what you want. Just keep my Rose out of this!" That evil smirk is enough to bend me.

How can a slut ruin my last goal in life? Sarah will pay for this. Nobody stands in the way of a man!

"Ok, I'll stay" I say.

"You will sleep with me tonight, and tomorrow you will move your stuff here. Do you understand me?" Sarah says. I nod.

She is out of her mind. I did not do great things to be controlled by this little girl. But my Rose cannot know about this affair. I am her hero, her moral example, and the man she truly loves. She won't ever want to see me, and it will kill me not to see her again.

"I'll wait for you in bed...." She stumbles up the stairs.

What do I do now? More sex? The tip of the sword is her weakness, sword, that's it... Eithan's dagger is in my pocket. Those beers and rum got to us, but now the solution is in my hand. The studio is dead silent, she must be deep asleep. The smell of acrylic paint hurts my head. Her red paints mix with glass shatters, like spilled blood...spilled blood?......

I have no other choice, my goals before anything   me, I, before anything   this is also to protect my beloved daughter   my

*dignity   I am a man, I have to do this   I don't
care   my rewards are worth it,   I am a man…..*

Sarah's door is open. My step becomes heavier and heavier, and my blood is cold as ice. The white blankets conceal her naked body. I aim the dagger at her, but my hands are stiff and heavy. Her snores are loud. What horrible insanity to listen to her for the rest of my days. I can't do this……

*Rose, get out of my head, let me do this, for both our sakes
you can't see this, it will hurt   please   leave now!
        you will hate me forever, I cannot bear that my entire body is a
stone, this girl has to go   her fault,   who told her to be in love
with an older man   she threatens my Rose, my sanity,
        the plans I made way before her mother brought her to this
horrendous world   why should   I   pay?   NO,
my happiness first……*

Her roaring snores rip my ears. It must be quick; otherwise, people will hear. My hands are soaking, and my heart pulls out of my chest. The moon's somber glimmer shines through the window. She moves, the moonlight illuminates the perfect place to strike her. That angelic skin, so sad it will rot. Where would it hurt less? Where would it kill her in one scream? In a single step, the floor makes an echoing squeal, she pops her eyes open. With force, I thrust the knife into her belly several times, and shut my eyes until her body relaxes. Sarah's flesh squirms as I extract the blade. She has beautiful intestines, all neatly arranged in the bed. Her last shriek rings in my ears, what an accomplishment. There is a gag in my throat, but I breathe and breathe. I drop the dagger and rush to chug some rum. The deed is not complete.

Sarah's cadaver is covered in blood. Her only family lives out of state, but what happens here must stay here…think, think… yes, art with art. Her storage room under the stairs is perfect to stuff a body. I carefully bring her corpse down the stairs, wrapped in the bed sheets, and shove her into the small spandrel. The bloody blankets and the art supplies cover her. I ensure that every drop of blood disappears with sanitizing wipes. Even the living room looks pristine; this is done with the utmost care. Hours pass…The evidence is hidden…finally the deed is complete.

An eerie shriek sounds through the studio. Is she alive? Or is this guilt? Her screams fade. Ok, I need to relax. She is dead and entombed. The bedroom is clear, the kitchen is clear. I'll leave the liquor bottles and red paint to make it seem like a suicide… I hope it looks like suicide; I hope. What have I done?

"You chose this, Sarah…." I slam the door.

Sherry's snores reverberate in the bedroom. The night is serene, my naked body shivers from the cold blankets. The bloody clothes are in the trash. Sherry must pay the price for marrying young: loneliness. Soon, I will be gone, forever. Sarah's shrieks bounce in my head and my heart begins to race. But it is over, and now my life will change.

Today marks a week since that deed. There is not an ounce of remorse because I stop at nothing to protect Rose. Love is a card game. That's all, you win or lose; I never lose. Sorry Sarah, it is all your fault. What a pity to die in your prime, but life goes on. A woman walks into the store with an infant. How lovely to see a proud mother. Sarah's pregnancy… the thought of it brings tears to my eyes. Her choice of abortion will haunt me forever. Eye for an eye is what keeps my sanity.

I am happy to have Rose, a perfect healthy girl. Rose should have been a boy. Much like me, strong, intelligent, educated, and fearless. Rose is my blessing, and as much as I hate to say it, Sherry is my bad blessing. The greatest gifts come with the most dreadful pain. Now I want to be alone. Rose has not been home lately. She must be busy with work or, hopefully, with school.

"Pa! Pa…" Rose's voice, a sound for my sour ears. I peek through the back door. She walks over with a smile strong enough to destroy any dreadful malady. A smile that no woman ever gave me, a smile I will never come across again in my life. She loves me, and everything I do is for her.

Two men in black suits enter the store with a stern demeanor. They slowly take off their shades and scan the store like robots. One of them wanders the store, and the other approaches the counter. My spine tingles, and my hairs rise. Did they find out?

"Greetings, I am Detective Lugo. We are looking for Ruben Rendar?" He asks.

"I am him."

The cop pulls out a tattered pink diary from his suit.

"Sarah Sahagun was found dead in her apartment a few days ago. We searched and found your name all over her diary."

Rubber wraps around my throat. How could I forget her stupid diary? That thing has all her deepest secrets, and now they threaten my peace.

"My God, my God. I did not know… I do not know anything of this, I…." The officer speaks over me.

"You are not under arrest, sir. However, we want to ask you some questions as part of our investigation."

I nod. After all, Sarah is not back from the dead to write about the deed. My integrity is to give my interpretation of the facts. It is all for my future, my well-being, and my Rose. Rose? She is gone. Rose shouldn't see this; it is horrible for her innocent eyes. The men step behind the counter, and I invite them to a chair. These are the facts…

5

For the first time in my miserable life, I leave home without telling my father how much I love him. He is my best friend, the person I trust the most. The thought of those officers stirs my guts like a whirlpool. But Laura is waiting for me, and Pa says, always keep a promise. Pa expects me to be the boy he never had. His advice is my protection and his love my refuge. I am made into his image. Pa is a strong-willed man, and he is all right; I can feel it. Laura must know my true feelings. It is a promise, and I keep all my promises. Regardless of the gray clouds and the dense fog that moves across the valley, this toxic relationship must end today. Pa needs me, and it is my duty as the firstborn daughter to care for my family above anything, even above love.

My relationship with Joseph is decrepit. Laura is my true love. My family won't understand me, but it is the truth. Why should I hide my feelings? Love is love. Joseph must know the truth. He cannot continue to hope for an unreal dream. Marriage is not for me because the thought of control makes me sick. I refuse to be like Ma. Women are more attuned to how a woman feels, but men just want pleasure or have too much pride or insecurities, like Joseph. Even masturbation is much better than him. If not Laura, then it is best to be alone. Alone is better. Joseph is my first time, but he finishes too quickly; he has a lot to learn. He knows how to put a smile on me with roses and chocolates. Perhaps I just love the idea of him. But that idea does not make me happy anymore. Pa taught me to be happy no matter what, and Joseph is no longer needed now that I know my true preferences. It is getting late, this road is endless, and my bug can only go so fast.

Joseph's car is parked on the street. The houselights are on, but he does not answer the door. Another knock…nothing. The tree branches rustle, cans rattle on the soulless street, and the wind gives an eerie blow. It is 1pm; Laura will meet me at 3pm. No matter what, Joseph cannot stall the inevitable.

Joseph finally swings the door open with a suspicious smirk. He covers my eyes and pulls me into the house. This won't take long, but the robust and delicious smell of spices travels up my nose. My mouth becomes watery, and food is my weakness. Joseph uncovers my eyes. Unbelievable! That is the red checkered tablecloth from *Comparis*--our favorite Italian restaurant--how cute! Two candles romanticize a dish of beef stew. He knows how much I adore the yellow hot sauce. My stomach begs for me to stay. How can I say no to this sad heaven? Joseph prepares a romantic dinner, unaware of my true feelings. I don't love him, but what about Pa's expectations? He wants me to marry, have children, and inherit the family fortune. Grandchildren would make Pa so happy, especially if it is a boy. I must respect my father's will, even if it means accepting Joseph. But what about me?

Joseph pulls out the chair for me and pours a glass of seltzer with a keen delicacy. He takes a few silent moments to say grace. I don't pray. This dinner is a financial sacrifice for a guy who works in auto maintenance. After the death of his parents, Joseph inherited his father's auto shop in Amourville and this little cottage. It is a challenge to stretch in this compact kitchen. That small grimy stove always makes me gag. His sink has dots of mold, and his small cabinets are stuffed with old mugs. The two light bulbs flicker, and the table shifts sideways because the legs are still broken. Joseph helps me remove my jacket, and my hair rises from the cold shock. Why is the living room dark? Hopefully not another surprise. I am Joseph's bad blessing. He has everything a woman wants, but I don't want him. He is great, but he does not make me happy.

The beef is soft as butter, the spicy cumin tickles my tongue, and the sweet, spicy chili ignites my entire mouth. The seltzer's bubbles pop in my burning taste buds; it is so good I almost choke. Joseph pats my back and serves me a glass of water. Joseph makes this more complicated, I can't say it, but I must. He sits in front of me and gives me the most charming smile, those smiles that imprint on you for life. But he should cry now than believe forever.

"Joseph, I must tell you something." He swiftly gets up from the table; this is awkward.

He returns with a little wooden box and goes on his knees. Please don't ask me that dreadful question, not now.

"Please open it." He says.

THE BAD BLESSINGS

My bracelet! Joseph, oh my sweet Joseph. My news are cruel, but I can't, I just can't. Tears gather at the corner of my eye......

what guy would keep a girl that rarely pays attention to him this food is delicious wonder how much this all cost him? But stupid Kashmir must you want everything that I have!
Now because of her, Joseph went through the trouble of fixing this and now now he glues the pieces of my bracelet and heart oh! This is spicy, but I just can't stop eating so good, he knows me... That is love right?
Maybe I should just stay with him, be a good daughter and make Pa proud Laura, what about Laura? But what will the town say my family cannot be in shame for my desires but......

He pecks my cheek, takes my hand, and places the bracelet on me with his soft pale hands. How could I break the person that stitches my broken memories?

"Joseph, you are everything a girl can want, but there is just something you must know...." He shushes me.

"Tell me later. Did you forget already?" He asks. I shrug.

"We are telling your parents our marriage plans." He says. A cold flash flood drops over my body.

"I, ah... yes, sorry, Joseph. Work and home have been pressuring me so much." I say.

"No worries, my business has not been great, but let's enjoy our dinner. Soon we will be a family."

He holds up his glass of seltzer for a toast. We cannot be a family because I don't love him… really, I don't… do I? I do, yet I don't…

Joseph wipes his mouth and rushes to the oven. He pulls out an enchanting pumpkin pie that opens a space in my stomach. He places the pie on the counter.

"No rush, just know that desert is looking at you." He chuckles, and I smirk.

Joseph then picks up after me. He serves me coffee, my most loved companion to pie. I just want pie and coffee. After this slice of heaven, I will break up with him and leave. What an amazing dinner; any woman would be head over heels for such a gentleman. Joseph does everything right except… sex.

I chug the last drip of my coffee and prepare my declaration. But again, another stumbling block. Joseph takes my hand and walks me over to the living room. It is hard to resist him, but why? Why? I am a bad bitch!

"Joseph, I don't know what to say for all this but…."

"I would do this and much more, my love."

"Then please do me a favor." I take a few steps back, "Joseph, the truth is…." He speaks over me, "Do you love me?" He says.

A knot tightens in my throat. I don't love him, but it will break his delicate heart. We have been together since high school. But I am only 19; he is 20, and our lives are in a different direction.

"I do…I…."

He gives me a kiss and rubs his hands on my hips. My muscles relax, and my lips pucker, but he rubs his wet lips in search of my tongue. We drop on the couch. Joseph turns on two lamps and caresses my body. My hairs rise, my body shivers……

What are these feelings, I can't be having these feelings, I don't love him, I don't like men but I just cannot bring myself to tell him
I only feel pity   Laura is going to be mad hopefully Pu is ok   he does not need more trouble   all he would want is for me to make him proud, but   Joseph please stop this……

"I love you, Rose." He whispers.

An earth-shattering rumble vibrates the house, and the first drops of water tap rhythmically on the roof. The drops turn into a torrent. I must leave.

"Joseph, you are sweet, but I just came over to confess something."

"Sorry, I just thought this would make you happy. Stay over…"

"I don't want to stay over, I…"

Lightning flashes, and with a blink of an eye, there is a blackout. The house is dead-silent except for the pitter-patter on the roof.

"Joe!" I yell, but no response.

A spine-tingling spasm stiffens my body. Even my phone has no service.

"Joseph!"

A flashlight emerges from the darkness, "Joseph, you could have said something!" My voice cracks.

"I wanted you to miss me."

"For a minute, I actually did."

"I'll light up the candles and make more coffee; you won't even be able to drive in this rain."

He has a point, but at least my heart won't crumble when his eyes flood like the rain. This blackout is my last opportunity. Joseph's lips continue to dominate my neck, his breath warms my cold skin, and his angelic hands massage every extremity of my body……

yes, rub it, so warm, the river, the butterflies   it tickles
just rub it   I don't know where he learned this
but just do it   his tongue penetrates my mouth
so hot to have a shirt on   oh the inside throbs
what a tease, he just rubs it but nothing   when
will he do it   when?!! there, there, go   these legs
are like jelly oh yes jelly,   almost there don't stop…yes!   You got
it! An unsettled ocean of sensations   oh yes!,   Laura!……

He moves with passion. He is a bull.

"Oh, I love you." I yell…… *but for Laura……*

We finish; I am so numb. A nap would be nice. But tonight, Joseph is another person, a man; I think I will stay… can't keep my eyes open, my heartbeat decreases…Joseph, what will I do? These contractions don't stop, but I can't be here; this is good…

The sun's rays tickle my eyes. My phone shows 7:30 am. Oh shit! I must leave! My shirt, where is my shirt! My hair! What will I tell Laura and Pa? Joseph wakes up.

"Joseph, consider this our last memory. It's over." I say. Joseph scratches his eyes, confused.

"I don't understand. You said you love me. Where are you going?"

"I realized I was wrong. I do not love you anymore. I need to be alone."

"Wait, what?"

"Thank you for everything. You made this very hard, but I came here to tell you we need to break up. I have someone else."

"You cold-hearted bit…."

"Bitch, I know, you deserve better."

He is speechless.

"We are just too young; in time, you will understand."

I grab my keys and open the door. His eyes get teary, but there is nothing I can do.

"Rose, if you walk out that door, you will regret it." He says.

If I turn back now, the little bit of love I have left will destroy me. But I can't. Like Pa, I must never turn back on my decisions. I love myself more than anything, so I shut the door.

Laura sends me a text to meet her at Dina's Café, in the heart of the big city. A swarm of yellow butterflies like the ones from El Coco River, surround me in a magical whirlpool. I squint and spot a black one. Strange yet beautiful. My hands shake as I reply.

The rich aroma of brewed coffee wakes my senses. The coffee shop is cozy with a vintage ambiance of the 50s. The seats are red, and the walls have old photographs of movie stars. Music plays from a jukebox, very classy and casual, just what I need after a dreadful night. There isn't many people, perfect for a love encounter.

"Rose…Rose." A lyrical voice sounds from across the restaurant.

Laura waves at me from a booth. She embraces me with her long thin arms and her perfect white smile. We gaze at each other with deep admiration and a vehement desire to taste our lips. Shyness overpowers me, what if people look, but she gives me an innocent peck. Laura is a chatterbox. I cannot help but admire her curly black hair, smooth ebony skin, delightful eyes of honey, and thin complexion. But is this love or admiration? I miss her presence around the office and her gentle strokes as I file court cases. Hopefully, we will have a bright future, like the couple that gets up from the table with a baby. How beautiful is it to forget gender and all social constructs and just be human.

Her advances are subtle yet demanding. She can come off as stern and impulsive, but she has a soft and forgiving side, which can be an issue for me. A person should be firm in their words no matter what, but she succumbs quickly, which makes me wonder if her backbone is real. Nonetheless, Laura listens to my troubles and values me as a person, much like Pa. Our love grows slowly, and my desire is to date her as much as possible.

"Rose? Are you even listening?" She giggles.

"Oh yes, sorry, I have many things to tell you."

"Me too. When can I meet your parents?"

"Soon, but what about your grandfather? You told me he was sick, right?"

"He is at a retirement home. If we move to the city, paying him a visit won't be too hard."

"Laura, if it was too difficult, we could have left this for another time."

"No!" She widens her eyes. "I don't want to lose you. We have put this off for a long time. It is time to formally present ourselves to your family." She asserts.

Laura knows what she wants, but it is a mistake to rush this courtship. We believe that if society and religion preach peace and love, then why do they censure our love, for love is love. Amourville needs to catch up with the rest of the world and accept the LGBTQ community. We should be allowed to love who we want. My family, however, is like a rock that blocks my river of feelings, my river of being. How will Amourville see this? Will Pa disown me? Will the inheritance go to my good-for-nothing sister? Will I be able to have dinner with my family with Laura at my side? We hold hands, and she blows me a kiss. The waitress brings our coffee.

Across the restaurant, a man sits on the bar stools. He squints at me with contempt, and he looks awfully familiar. Is that one of Pa's friends… Mr. Eric! What is he doing here? Coincidence, or conspiracy? His pale blue eyes rip through me… his eyes, eyes, what do eyes want with me? Are they following me? My blood freezes, his eerie eyes want to destroy what I truly am.

I let go of Laura's hand. She scowls and turns back to look at Mr. Eric. This is embarrassing. Now, my personal life will spread through Amourville. It will break my Pa's heart. That can't happen, not my Pa. Perhaps it is best to terminate this date. Laura turns around with a sullen expression.

"How do you know you love me, Rose?"

She crosses her arms. I pour more cream into my cup.

"I would not be here, Laura."

"Are you afraid?"

"I am not afraid of anything or anyone!"

"Then who is that man?"

"Laura, let's talk about important things."

"How do I know you won't be ashamed when I meet your parents?" She raises her voice, and the customers turn to look at us.

"Calm down. Don't you think it is too soon to meet my family?"

"Rose, I left my family for you!" Her voice cracks.

"I am just not ready, sorry, at least I am telling you now."

"Really bitch! You either tell your parents, or I'll end my life!

She slams her hand on the table. Some customers get up and leave.

"Relax, or I leave." I say.

"My love or my death!" She raises her eyebrow.

Laura is beautiful, but I can't stand pushy people. Her insecurity is also a turn-off. Perhaps this relationship will not work. Besides, love is not my priority.

"Why do you cry?" I ask.

"Sorry, I didn't mean to be so odd… I am just afraid to lose you… was I too odd? Yes, or no, tell me, was I odd?"

"O-o-o-k…everything is happening all at once. I do love you. And… you… are not odd, just..."

"Then promise me we will meet your family…swear to me."

Laura reaches for my hand and gives me a tight grip, and her eyes become glossy.

> *......she is really sprung in love,*   *Why?*
> *She just needs validation,*   *I really can't be with someone needy*
> *seeking validation*   *I really should get going to work but   we*

both left important things behind then   I guess we can try but what
a nosy society,   why was he here, why does
he care! What will I tell Pa now?   I am too deep into
this, I rather be alone,   love is not for me......

"I... I swear." I mutter.

Her long smile squeezes the tears out of her eyes, and she kisses my hand. Then, she moves next to me.

"I promise to control myself. I just wish to be the man and protect the woman I love. I would do anything to not lose you...my love." She hugs me.......

The man?!   She is totally out of her fucking mind!   I am no little dumb girl!   Just because she is 20 and going to college?! No!   No!   You are the boy I never had, that's what my Pa told me,   I am not a little girl anymore shit, look at the time, I must leave......

"It's ok, love, I completely understand. Now I must get to work." I say.

Laura reaches for my arm in the parking lot and holds me against my car. I resist, but she has some strength, and it would be stupid to make a scene. Too many eyes can report this to my family. But butterflies fly in my stomach as the sun shines upon her dreamy eyes. We kiss passionately, with no shame and no rush. Each glance is a drug from which the only cure is more and more of her. Our tension dissuades, and we agree to make plans. Although she is beautiful and kindhearted,

I hate pressure. I do things when they are convenient, not when someone tells me. Laura might not be the one for me.

My head is a blender, my mouth is salty, and the urge to vomit keeps me by the toilet. My period is late this month. Perhaps all the stress from work, the strange things in my family, and Laura's pressure. But this pregnancy test is just to get a peace of mind. These are the most eternal five minutes of my life…the control line, ok, and the results? A manly body like mine can't have kids. If it is negative, I need to avoid all this stress. If it is positive, I cannot have this kid. But that is murder, it's wrong, disgusting, and my Pa will be devastated. What a bad blessing, kids were never in my plans, never!......

What?!!!...... +...... this is false, it must be,   how can I be pregnant?!   The night of the thunderstorm!
Joseph   He planned it!   What will I tell my parents?   We did it, but that was like a long time ago I don't know   no, no,   this is a false positive   ok, ok Web Md says ok, yes to retest there are false positives   what the hell am I saying!! Ok maybe just some Advil and that's it I go work and … and   that's it I will be ok, but lesbian and pregnant!   It's   ok   I'll   test   again; Joseph had a condom   I don't remember......

After all these strange happenings in the family, Pa deserves an excellent homemade breakfast. I serve him his coffee, extra bold, extra sugar, and cream, but he doesn't even touch it. Ma always upsets him, or maybe he is thinking about those cops. But with Pa, the wrong question at the wrong time will anger him for days. This is the wrong moment to give him crap about my uncertain pregnancy. I am not pregnant, but if I am, he does not need to know. It is the only thing I will keep from him. Pa gets up, absentminded.

"Your food, daddy!" He taps his head and sits down to eat. Pa usually devours steak and eggs, but he barely touches it this time.

"What is wrong, Pa?"

"What have we done to deserve all this? All these things happen, and they have no explanation."

Sometimes I think the events at the Estrada ranch have some connection to the strange happenings in my family, but I am not sure, I don't like to overthink things. No… I am just going crazy, too much stress. A pressure forms in my chest just by those thoughts, the twins…am I responsible? Maybe I am making this about me when it shouldn't. But just when things seem good for us, a calamity strikes. The store is not doing so good, I am dealing with relationships, and Pa is depressed. Our house has a putrid smell of dead rat, even if Ma always cleans it. If God exists, what blessings are these?

"Pa, did we do something wrong?" I stroke his head.

"No, we are just slaves to the store." He chuckles. "I was a renowned veterinarian, I studied with Dr. Lorenzo Santamaria, the greatest doctor that ever lived in California, and now I run a store. Some dream, huh… but I guess things happen…."

A shadow moves in the corner of my eye. Grams stands by the doorway and then walks back to the living room. Hopefully, she forgets this conversation before she instigates Ma.

"This family won't fall, which is why I will take a drastic decision." He says, confident. My heart accelerates.

"What decision?"

"It is nothing bad, love, I promise." He kisses my forehead. "How's everything with you, my love? And Joseph?"

Pa does not need to know about my breakup, nor does he need to know about Laura. A relationship is likely not ideal at this moment. My family needs me first; I want to be someone in life, not someone's little wife. They need someone to be proud of, and that is me. Love is perhaps not for me, at least not now. My phone vibrates; it's a text message from Laura: *Hey sweetie, don't forget to tell your parents… then let me know… miss you, love you!* Her persistence is a hateful virtue.

"My dream is to give you, our inheritance. Then, when you have a child, he will keep our legacy alive. I might not live to see it, but you and your son will make the Rendars proud." He says.

"All I want is to make you proud, Pa."

"Believe in yourself but only after reflection." He says. I get up and walk towards the window, the fresh air stiffens my balmy skin......

Our garden is beautiful, a simple glance at it relaxes me, but Pa places a burden on me give it to Kashmir! She is still his daughter, not me me carry the name of the family. How can I be so selfish? My father deals with demons and I debate whether love exists or not I am selfish yes I am

but what about my needs what is wrong with my family? Laura loves me, but does she? Or does she just want someone to control, she just wants to be a man she wants validation

my poor Joseph, you were always there, how could I?

No! I don't like men, perhaps I am destined to be alone... forever, I do believe in myself, and I believe that my family comes first, I cannot let father down, but I thought he was perfect, all these years I thought Ma was the problem poor Ma, how could he? I might have done the same but still, if I were Ma I would hate him, I would never want to see him again

what about my choices, my life? Pa why, why did you do that? That was dirty, I love you but that was so fucken dirty, that is why I don't like guys I cannot, can I?......

The brisk wind blows through the veranda and picks the leaves off the ground. A chorus resonates in the waving trees, a soothing song to ease the troubles that infiltrate my mind. As the wind blows in a rhythmic howl, my nose stiffens at the smell of tobacco. Grams sits in her rocking chair with her usual cigar and gives me a smile.

"Your Papa is right. You are our only hope." A cloud of smoke covers her face. I kiss her head and walk away.

"Even the wind changes, my dear…." She shouts. Grams is right. If the wind changes, then I need to change all the sadness into happiness. Family first… I will make things change.

Where can Joseph be on a Saturday afternoon? He won't even reply to my texts, I don't blame him. I drive over to his auto shop. My life is too complex. People either expect too much from me or hide from me. This is the price of independence, masculinity, or perhaps the price for dishonoring my family. Is this love? I hope not; this is stressful and unnatural, and it feels like a betrayal to who I really am. I don't love anyone because others don't feel what I feel. Only my Pa does.

Joseph's shop is empty. A voice echoes from the oil-disposing chamber.

"Joseph, it's Rose!" My voice fades into the chamber. Joseph emerges with oil spots on his face and his gasoline suit.

"Never thought I'd see you again." He snorts with his hands over his hips.

"It's not about me; I have something to show you."

I pull out a document from my purse and hand it to him. He snatches it, but in a matter of seconds, his mouth drops, his eyes widen, and his hands shiver.

"We are done, but it is your right to know." I say.

"How do I know this is my child?"

"I don't like men, but you were my first and only, Joseph."

"Honestly, I have a girl pregnant; she has no job. So, she needs me more than you."

"I don't need anything from you, don't ever look for me again nor this child. Just know that somewhere you have a kid that will never know you exist."

Expectations are just the flip side of deception, and I am tired of so many expectations; this is the last one. I never want to see Joseph again.

"But it is still my child!" He shouts.

"It won't even know your name. I loved you, but you proved that men do not want love. They only want to love the experience."

Joseph attempts to give me a hug, but I step away. It hurts. I can't deny it. He could have been my love, but why cry for impossible things? It's better to suffer for things that I can control.

"We will never see each other again. I mean it."

"Rose!"

I hop into my car and drive off. No matter how much I try to cry, no tears come out. No desire to look back and wave at him, no desire to thank him for the laughs, the cries, the good times in school, the shoulder to cry on, the food, and the sex…to thank him will be a mistake. This is not a mistake. We are taking different paths in life, that is all. These are my choices, and it feels good to own up to them. Laura blows up my phone with calls and messages. What a nuisance; maybe she is not that important to me.

Meet me at the pier. I must speak to you urgently, I text her. Moments later, she replies… *Ok, love.* Laura must also know about this child and the fate of our relationship. If this is the Rendar's pride, I embrace it before anything, even Laura. Family first, I am absolute. I need no one.

A dense fog accumulates over the bay. My hair rises from the frightening horn on the lighthouse, and the icy mist tickles my face. The wind blows, and tranquility overcomes me.

Suddenly, two hands cover the peaceful view. After a second, the hands lift, and Laura's beauty radiates amid the grey fog. Our icy lips touch, she wants more affection, but I take a few steps away. Her smile gradually shifts to a frown.

"We cannot be together, Laura. I am pregnant. It is my ex's, but we broke up." Laura pulls her hair and then leans against the railings to gasp for air.

"I don't love him, but it wouldn't be right for you to be…." She speaks over me.

"Why did you do it?" She asks.

The reason still puzzles me. Seduction, lust, maybe the enchantment of a first love. Does not matter anymore, not even to her.

"I was blind. That is all I can say. These are all my mistakes, and I am facing my consequences."

Laura looks out the bay. She is clouded in fog and sadness. For the first time in my life, pity grabs me, but my eyes still can't shed a tear.

"We can raise the child together." She says.

"My family won't approve."

"What the fuck! Who do you love more, your family or me?"

"Laura, my family just suffered a terrible death! Have a heart!" My voice cracks.

"I suffered a death to be with you too, and there will be one more!" Her red eyeballs bulge. "I love you, but if I cannot have you, then there is no point for me to live."

She moves her long legs to the outer side of the railings. Laura is extreme, but this is crazy. I can't deal with her, but she can't die for me.

"Laura, stop! Don't make this difficult."

I grab hold of her thin body. She hugs me tight.

"This is a blessing. Stay with me. We will make this child happy." She whispers in my ear.

"This is a bad blessing. I promised my family, and I must keep it."

"What about us?"

"I will always love you, Laura. And because I love you, I can't put you through this."

I try to kiss her, but she pushes me away.

The sun's rays rip through the grey clouds and form a faded rainbow. The mist falls over the shining rainbow like the tears that fall off Laura's face.

"Promise me one thing," I say. "Please don't hate me. But if you find love, don't let go of it."

"Will I ever see you again?" She asks.

"I hope so."

She nods, and we kiss passionately. But something tells me this is not the last time we will see each other. I do not want to leave her, but my family always comes before me. The fog overpowers the sun, the rainbow dies, and the pier lights give a ghastly blue glimmer. I love Laura, but Laura is now a blue shadow. I have nothing to lose. I am free.

THE BAD BLESSINGS

Kashmir makes a nerve-racking scream from the bathroom. My body freezes; that amorphous shadow with a long pipe-like hat, two red dots, and about seven feet tall stands by the bathroom. It seems to look for something, then it slides along the wall. It moves its head but does not notice me! The shadow's head protrudes from its body and moves around the room like a hose. I can't scream. The shadow now locks eyes on me. Now it retracts its head back, and slides to the bathroom……

> *this is not true, I don't believe in this,   ok,   I   am   just tired, I did stuff I was not supposed to   ok*
> *I don't believe in God, but I don't believe in the devil everything is my fault   I am the only one that can fix it*
> *now enough horseshit   enough Rose!   You are a man and a woman, now stop seeing shit and get back to reality!*
> *But that shadow, I know it,   it has been following me forever, I saw it somewhere,   it always comes up!   What is it?   Does it want to hurt my family?   What is it?*
> *Kashmir!……*

My numb feet plod through the room. Finally, I open the bathroom door, and Kashmir rushes to her bed and covers herself with a blanket. That awful thing is strangely familiar. Memories flash---the small window, Pa asleep, the cart, that shadow! I must be tired, too many things, or it's the pregnancy hormones. Perhaps some food will calm my nerves.

The pungent aroma of onion permeates the kitchen. Bubbles gather around the sizzling plantains, and the oil sputter tingles my ears. I reach for one, but the sprinkles of oil burn my skin. Ma skillfully removes the plantains from the skillet and places them in a bowl. Once the table is set, Ma says grace. I shut my eyes and peek through my eyelids and notice my Ma's countenance. It is more sullen than pious.

"Deliver us from evil…amen." Ma barely touches her food. I devour it.

Prayer is such a selfish thing. What can a powerful being do for one family? So many people pray and pray… nothing ever happens. Grams pours herself coffee—she is not religious either—and serves herself three cardamom cakes. We eat dinner in solemn silence. Ma must know about my child, mainly since I will not abort.

"Mother, grandmother…" They stare at me.

"It is only us three, but we are still a happy family, and I love you both, which is why I know this will bring you hope and happiness, since the Rendars lost it. I am pregnant…."

Mother drops her mouth and utensils. Grams chuckles and gives her cardamom cake several dips into her coffee.

"Joseph is the father, but it was unintentional. I will care for the child. Joseph has his own family now."

"But… who will you marry? What will everyone say?" Ma says.

"I don't care about anyone's opinion Ma. I don't wish to be with anyone."

Ma places her hands over her head. Grams is nonchalant. Perhaps she perceives something that none of us can see. Perhaps she knows this child is a good omen.

"You must be married! Amourville will say Rose Rendar is a whore!" Ma yells.

"I don't like men, mother. I like women. I waited too long to tell you, but this is who I am."

Her face turns purple, then there are shades of green, and finally, she is pale and stiff as a corpse. Finally, she tightens her fists, ready to strike me. I have never seen this side of Ma, but I am proud and happy for this moment.

"She was a girl from work. I met her when I was with Joseph. But I am not with her, all to keep my honor."

Mother tosses her plate of food at the wall. Grams leaves to the living room. Ma whimpers and then goes on her knees to pray. Grams walks back into the kitchen.

"Do you love her?" Grams says.

"Yes…"

Ma grabs the table knife and points it at her neck.

"Your father and I worked so hard, and this is how you pay us!" Ma says.

"Mother, in this entire family, I am the only one that appreciates what father did! I know what you did, so don't pretend you are holy! We are imperfect, and if you truly love me, you will accept me."

Ma drops the knife and sits in her seat.

"I made a promise to my father, and I am keeping it, with or without you."

There is deep silence, except for the rapid breathing of Ma. She then puts her head down on the table, and Grams sits next to her. She strokes her back.

"Rose..." Ma keeps her face down, "why did you leave her?" She asks.

"For my family and my child." I say.

Mother walks up to me. She has a stern expression but then bursts into tears and gives me a tight hug. I did it... it is best to show what is in my heart before it is too late, now I feel free and accepted.

"My Rose, my everything, our only hope." She cries. "Does Kashmir know, dear?" Ma says.

"No."

"I hope she was here, I went to the clinic to get her test results, and they are not good." Ma says.

THE BAD BLESSINGS

"What do the results say, Ma?"

"I'll show them to you." Ma heads over to the room.

Grams gets up and rubs my belly.

"Finally, a blessing. It is up to you to decide if it is a good or bad blessing. It's up to you, savior...." Grams heads over to the living room with her mug.......

I want to die this night,   at sea perhaps, facing the sunset... sunset where pain is but a thought   my mind a dove over the heaven   did Ma accept it or not?   A deep silence a deep loneliness a deep sadness   but I rather end up alone than shame my family and break my promise,   I don't know what kind of blessing   but I know my child is a blessing for this great family   Father, I know I made you proud I will keep this promise   and this child will keep the Rendars alive, forever sometimes we have to be brave   sometimes it is better to be honest regardless of the pain   for in truth there is still opinion   and everyone finds comfort in their opinion   Ma will find her comfort, I can already hear Ma sobbing, Kashmir, stupid little sister   who knows what she has, time give us a temporary crown, makes us believe we have power   no we really don't life is not ours, life simply likes to play with us   but in this chaos,   a dancing star will arise......

6

That is the truth, the plain truth. All great things come to an end. Too many fights and arguments, and after a month, we completely cut ties. The officers exchange doubtful glances. The young detective opens her hideous pink diary. The mere thought of all her feelings and adventures with me twists my guts. He turns through several pages and points to the last entry, which dates three days before the murder. They scowl at me.

"This is my side of the story. There is nothing to hide, gentlemen." I say……

Ok think, think Ruben   if you don't get out of this one you won't retire in peace! My little Rose, how I hope she did not see this   no,   she probably thought I was busy and left   yes she is a good girl, always makes me proud   what the hell is this kid looking around for?   Does he expect to find her panties?   Her body parts! Ok, what do I say, keep calm, they need to leave, it is bad for business, what will the town people say   As long as my Rose does not suspectyes wise guy, yes ok,   deny, play dumb, whatever they say, they need to leave   That diary does not state I killed her   it is just about her   it does not prove anything……

The veteran detective pulls out some old photos of our vacation in Nicaragua. Those fun times return to bite me in the ass.

"Where were you the night of the murder?" The veteran asks.

"I… I was at my friend's house. We play poker on some nights."

"Good alibi…" The young detective says.

"Do you know if anybody wanted to kill her? Any enemies? Trouble at work? Family issues?" The veteran asks.

"Oh, well, I don't know, she did have guys after her, but she was faithful to me. But I don't think it is related…."

The cocky young detective diligently takes note of everything. But he keeps glancing around the store. It must suck to be a novice, an idiot.

"We were having an affair, but she was into herself. I think she had three boyfriends before me, but it has been years, I don't know." I say.

"Why did you break up with Sarah Sahagun? Did your wife ever find out?"

"No, she did not. And well, I already told you, we just fought too much, and she hated that I couldn't perform."

"She never mentioned performance in her diary." The older detective says.

"I have a sexual dysfunction detective. Soon you might experience that too."

The veteran snorts and scrolls through the diary, and the youngster hesitates his notation.

"Write it down, young man. You are not getting younger." I say. He looks at me from head to toe, young fool.

"So that is why you broke up?" The veteran asks.

"I am old and couldn't keep up with a young girl. I… I don't know what else to say. This is all too shocking!" I cover my face with my hands and pretend to whimper.

The older detective closes the diary. His partner wraps up his notes and gives another glance at the store. They seem convinced by my great testimony.

"Excuse my question, detective, but her only family lives far away. How did you discover she was murdered?" I say.

"A neighbor said they saw a man exit her studio, but they couldn't identify him." The veteran says.

I cover my mouth. I am close, too close, but got to keep playing the part. Soon, I will be in the woods, where nobody can find me.

"Instead of that diary, check my records. I cannot drive at night."

The veteran nods at the youngster, and the novice jots it down.

"We will review these notes and your testimony. We will be in touch, Mr. Rendar."

We all shake hands. The young one, a cocky son of a bitch, sneers at me before he walks out. The older one stays behind and wanders around the store.

"Do you need anything else, detective?"

He grabs a syringe. What the hell is a syringe doing there? Stupid Sherry.

"What are these for?" He says.

"They are antibiotics for livestock. I was a veterinarian." He nods, "What would happen if you injected this into a human?"

"Never tried it, kill them perhaps, or maybe get them a little better."

He nods and tosses the syringe on the shelve. "Sorry for the intrusion. Have a pleasant day."

What an awkward investigation, animal medication on humans? He probably thinks I am a drug dealer or something. The more confused they are, the better. It gives me time to arrange some documents and get out of here. What is this? Oh crap! Eithan's dagger! This can take me to jail. I must return this dagger before those goons return with more questions. Sherry walks into the house; church is over by now. I close the store and switch the will return signage to 2:00pm. Two hours should be enough to cover this mess.

Eithan gradually opens the door, his hair spikes up like thorns, his pale face drags like an old rag, and he looks at me with bloodshot eyes. Sewage comes out of his mouth. He leans his head on the door. Typical hangover, I wish I could be him. Alcohol is a captivating escape.

I reveal his dagger, and his languid eyes light up. Eithan snatches the dagger of my hand and squints at it for a moment. He scratches his head and breaks into laughter. More disoriented than usual, he must be on drugs too. He then splashes a water bottle on his face and gasps for air. Eithan's friendship is not a good alibi.

"Refreshing! I am ok, my friend. Talk to me…."

"I need your help, friend." I pat his shoulder.

He nods and cracks up again. The newspaper boy tosses *The Rambler*—Amourville's local newspaper—on the steps. Eithan pretends to read it, but he moves his head sideways.

"So, Ruben?" He mutters.

"If the police come to question you, I need you to tell them I was with you on November 3rd."

He puts down the newspaper at stares at me, baffled.

"What you do?"

"Honestly I…"

"Oh my god! It's ok, we have a drink. Ya!"

"No, it's ok, thanks, I have to get back to the store, and this is serious."

"Ok, only me, no like…" He lights a cigarette and continues to glance at the newspaper.

Eithan crumples the sides of the newspaper. He swings back and forth, hysterical. He coughs and coughs and exchanges glances between me and the newspaper.

He shows me the headline: *Woman Mysteriously Found Dead in her Studio.* An anvil drops on my chest, and my teeth chatter.

"That is Sarah!" He yells.

I snatch the newspaper, and without a doubt, it is her studio and her wrapped body under the spandrel.

"A man kill her. It was you Ruben! You running!" He grabs me by the shirt.

"I… I don't know anything about this!" I shove him away.

"Yes, yes, you do! You... break up... her! You kill... not Sherry!?"

He slurs his words but yells at the top of his lungs. I better leave before his nosy neighbors call the police.

"No, we just broke up that night. I don't know anything. Can you help me?"

Eithan's red eyeballs bulge out, he can barely maintain his balance. It is pointless to make agreements with this idiot. Perhaps it is best to return when he is sober. He will likely forget; otherwise, I might need to kill him.

"Ruben! Why do you run? That means it was you!" He yells. I run back to cover his mouth.

"Shut up, you drunk. I already told you it was not me. If they ask you, all you must say is I was here with you, that's all!" He pushes me back.

"No! No! We friends, no-kill bitches, we love them!"

I rush back to my car, but Eithan limps after me.

"Murderer, he is here. He duns it, murderer!"

The neighbors step out from the sound of his horrible squeals.

My truck is across from his house. I jump onto the busy street, but he comes behind me like a zombie with the newspaper in his hand. Honks and trails of acrid smoke block the way to my truck. Then there is a clear, lasting only a few seconds. Eithan limps onto the street, frantic. He then loses his balance. An 18-wheeler honks several times and its tires screech.

"Hey, go back!" I yell. Eithan is completely dazed.

The truck loses control and runs over Eithan. His guts spill all over the street. The neighbors scream, the traffic jams, and people gather around the scene. Eithan's torn hand is but a few feet away from me, open yet still useless. The crowd points at me. Should I leave or stay? He is a friend under the influence but… it isn't my fault, there is nothing to worry about. But Sarah's death is in the newspaper! It won't be long until Dillon and Eric find out. I must leave; society is not safe anymore. Eithan is a casualty of my goals. I am sorry… friend.

The store reopens at 2:35pm. A little behind schedule, but at least not too many people show up at midday. My truck is at the end of the driveway. Nobody will notice it there. My forehead is drenched in sweat. Customers walk in to browse but leave as soon as they see me. Do they know? But what do they know? Eithan lives far from here, and they can't track me down. People scowl at me regardless of my smile. Something is out of place, and my body shivers. There is a bottle of whiskey under the register counter. Alcohol is always there for the bad moments; it soothes my dry throat. Oh lord, it burns my mouth away! Almost done, just a few more shots, work, work, issues, stupid people, again and again.

My life here is over, love is over, family is over, friends are gone, and to hell with this town. In the woods, I will reflect on life and die as a philosopher.......

This whiskey is good, almost done, more no!　My Rose, where is my Rose?!　　She is the only family that is not over, never! I　must speak with her!　　　Soothing,　relaxing,　but the room floats like a boat, my eyes lag,　I am trying to see　damn it is good
　　　call Sherry so she can close,　　Sarah why?　　The boat sinks, help!　　Hey I am super low close to the floor, this is a good drink,　sure why not, a little nap......

It is now four weeks since the investigation. The authorities classify Eithan's death as suicide; I am clear, sorry...friend. My family is not the same anymore. Business is bad, we can't live together, and I see things like shadows. Life is not the same. So why get out of bed and deal with the same routine? Sherry's big pendulum clock slows down time; it drives me nuts. This claustrophobic living room does not let me breathe. Sarah's wails haunt me at every moment. The stench of mold revives my plan of life in the woods. What the hell am I still doing here? It won't be long until Sherry returns and nags me about the store and her mother. I cannot live like this. I must pack, but even my Rose avoids me. I can't go without giving her the inheritance.

My drawer is half open. Sherry's disgusting habit never gets old---always going through my stuff. There is an old photograph within the mess. It is a picture of Rose and I with

Thomas's family outside the ranch. That strange lady, she gives me the creeps.......

Alice, never heard from her again, she was great, asking me over and over to run away with her, not my fault Thomas had impotency

oh but those times in the barn, and her old room, she was an amazing girl   but my face? It fades everyone is visible except me and Rose, she was so little, but always by my side, it will hurt to leave her

that strange lady,   she would stare and stare,   everything Alice did, she was there yelling at her   Thomas never cared about Alice

her yellow eyes like a demon, her creepy necklace always mumbling something around me,   my head would spin after being around her, that woman must have done something, I don't know, I am not superstitious but evil must exist for good to exist, otherwise what explanation is there for all the bad things happening in the family,   what is wrong with my family!   Alice,   if I would have listened to you life would be different, we would have kids

that woman, the more I look the more I shiver maybe she cursed me!......

Poor Thomas, it sucks to have a life without love. Alice, what a beautiful girl. No…passions aside, I am a responsible father. My life is crappy, but it is better than Thomas'. I have a trustworthy daughter, and she is above the love of any woman. The past is not an illusion, and the consequences are proof that the past will forever haunt me, unless I do something. Rose needs to know the truth, even if it hurts her. My consciousness must be clean before I leave.

"Pa, breakfast is ready." Rose yells from the kitchen.

The same tiny nasty little kitchen, it sometimes smells like coffee, sometimes like food, sometimes like… I don't even know. We barely can move around here, even my mind is clearer than this hole.

Rose serves my favorite dish. *Ruben… Ruben…Ruben…* Who is that! She is here, that old woman is in the kitchen… her voice is in my ear. No, no…I am just stressed, but I can hear her, or is it my head messing with me? My appetite is gone. Coffee will suffice. These voices can't be an excuse to stop this critical moment. This is for my daughter and my family, and a true man must do anything to care for his family, even if it is the last thing I do. But what if Rose rejects my gift? What if she is not what I think she is? What if there is a curse in the Rendar family? I don't care. Rose is a loyal and fearless young lady. She won't let me down; she never will.

"My love, there is something important I must tell you."

She nods with such deep innocence. I can't give her this burden, but there is no other choice. I love her, but even my need is more significant than my love for Rose.

"I am passing the Rendar fortune to you. This house, the store, our acres of land, and our entire savings will be under your name."

Rose widens her eyes and gasps for air. She takes a long sip of her coffee.

"Really, Pa?"

"Yes, I am sick, old, and there is nobody in the family I trust but you."

Rose gets up and stares out the window, silent and unemotional. Why doesn't she respond? What is she thinking?

"One day, you will marry Joseph. Then, your children will carry our name, and your descendants will continue my legacy, our legacy of honor."

She still doesn't respond. Rose is stubborn, but she holds me at the highest level of love and respect... I can convince her.

"I cannot do this, Pa. I am too young and afraid to dishonor the family."

"Rose, you are an adult now, and this is the only way to take the shame away from us."

She saunters around the tiny kitchen, absentminded. Rose is the most complicated person to convince. She does not listen to reason, and her cold heart houses the cruelest emotions. Her little soft side is my only hope.

"Rose, nothing is more dishonorable than a man bringing shame to his family like me." A rain of fear pours over my body. "I plan to spend my last days in the woods away from all the pain I caused."

"What are you talking about?"

"While at the Estrada ranch, Alice and I had an affair. I went to be away from your mother. Do you remember?"

Her mouth drops, and her face turns pale. She turns back to the window.

"I am sorry, Rose. It has consumed me all these years. Nobody knows this but you." She does not respond… "Rose?"

She begins to whimper and covers her face with her hands. It hurts me, like acid to a wound. My nights of passion are not worth the pain of seeing my daughter cry for me. The masks on my face are never the same. They change in every role I play in my life. But now, I don't know what mask to change into. All this for a woman?

"Please… for…give me, you are the only person I would ever ask for forgiveness, ever!" I slur.

She turns and looks at me with a sullen countenance.

"All these years, I thought you were a hero." She whispers.

I lower my head and wipe the cold sweat off.

"I cannot accept father, you hurt mother, and you hurt me as well."

"I know, love, and that is why I must leave. It has always been my plan. I even told you this as a little girl, remember? You must accept the inheritance. I am dying."

THE BAD BLESSINGS

"No! Give it to Kashmir!"

"Rose! Stop!" She stops at the door frame… "Set your stubbornness aside!"

"Shame or not, you are my firstborn, the one I dreamed of giving this to. If you accept this, your loyalty will take our shame away. I want to find the meaning of life and die in peace. If you were there for me before, then be here for me now when I need you the most."

She turns towards me with her head down.

"I cannot clear your mistakes." She says.

"Before this happened, I had already chosen you to carry our name. Please, my love, you can save the family."

"I am sorry, father, but…I c-a-n-n-o-t… accept such a responsibility." Her voice cracks.

Stupid little girl, she thinks she knows it all. Who will really love her? Rose is difficult, but I can read her. She wants to take the inheritance, but something torments her. Perhaps she did something shameful, something she knows will dishonor me. There isn't any time to dissect her feelings. Frankly, I don't care. My goal is for her to sign the inheritance papers. Once done, I will be free to live the rest of my days in peace. No matter how much I love her, this foolish girl will not ruin my final goal.

"Rose, I don't want to be forgiven. I want to be understood. You and I, we are alike. We don't let anything stop us. Please accept, don't be my obstacle. My past is a grave without a body..."

"I am sorry, I can't... I..."

"Rose... we either save ourselves or destroy ourselves. You choose. But I expect you to accept...."

She smirks and heads out of the house. Rose will accept, but I can't leave without her signature. Her words spill the bit of innocence left in her. Whatever consumes her mind will push her to accept; I know her.

This is my last day in this prison—it can't be freedom when everyone suspects you and when your family falls apart—by tonight, there will be no more work, no more Sherry, no more stupid people, no more Pauline, no more Kashmir, and no more friends. My Rose will be gone too. Even freedom has a price, but it is good to be proud of pain. In pain, we remember how perfect we have become...

Henry Miles, the only notary public in town, sits like an ancient entity on his throne-like chair. He presses one finger into his typewriter at a time. The claustrophobic burgundy walls have mildew between the cracks, but his neatly arranged books alleviate the decrepit aura. His desk is a neat mess with sprinkles of coffee, a layer of dust bends his old quill, and his ceiling is covered in brown stains. Gladly, we are not here on a rainy day. The office has a deafening silence, except for that pendulum clock above him. Each eerie dial makes me cringe. His secretary, a delicate blonde girl around 20, languid and slow, hands him some documents. Rose is serene and a bit aloof.

Miles clears his desk with a swing of his hand. He methodically spreads the documents and nods over them.

"Ruben Rendar." He says.

"Why is a… girl getting a family inheritance?"

Rose and I exchange glances.

"Because I decided to." I say sternly.

He returns to his ponderous typing. My patience boils. Miles examines the documents for an eternal minute, then gazes at Rose several times.

"But she is a girl?"

"And?!" Rose says.

"Love, please. I am paying you for a service, Mr. Miles."

Miles tosses the documents on his desk.

"My conscience hurts. It is against custom. How can a woman have such large properties?" He says.

"Mr. Miles, you were recommended by close friends." I lean closer, "You either do this, or the town will know you falsify documents. How's that for a clean conscience?"

He scowls at us. Rose tries to get up, but my grip detains her.

"Women just don't know their place. Oh, God help us!" He says.

The wise fool hands the documents to Rose. She looks at me with profound confusion.

"Sign them, you want the property, then do manly things," Miles says.

With her shivering hands, Rose seals her fate. Miles snatches the documents and spills them on the floor. It seems accidental, but he likely wants to prove a point. His secretary rushes to pick up the papers. He smirks, and she returns to her desk without question. We all get up and shake hands. Rose keeps her chin up and gives him a disdainful glare.

"Never mind him. He is old school." The secretary says.

"I don't blame him; it is Amourville," I reply.

Outside the office, Rose gives me a hug. This is probably the last one before I retreat to the woods.

"I promise you, the Rendar inheritance is safe with me."

"It is an honor to have you as my child, Rose."

"Now I must take care of something on my own, for us and the family too." She kisses my forehead, and I stroke her arm.

"Remember, there is no great pain, regrets, or pleasure. Everything is forgotten, even love. Love yourself before anything."

She smiles, a smile someone gives you before they die in peace, a smile that carries a painful joy that I will miss forever.

Solitude is what a man needs at the end of his life. The petrichor cleanses the smog from my nose, and each breath elevates my body like a leaf. The cabin is ghost-silent except for the howling wind and the birds' tweets. The small boxy room has a smokey humid stench that tickles my throat. I run my fingers over the wooden walls. Pieces of mortar pinch the tip of my finger, but the logs are still stable. The family photos are covered in dust and there are cobwebs all over the stone chimney. The burnt chimney… I can hear scary stories that chill the foggy nights. On the blue velvet sofa… Rose and Kashmir fall asleep with me. My desk is next to the only window where faint sunlight creeps into the lonesome red living room. Sherry's abandoned kitchen fills the room with the smell of freshly baked bread. The beds upstairs are cozy and neat. The cold stillness crawls up my spine, did someone sleep here? Is anybody else here? Footsteps echo on the bottom floor. I rush downstairs, but the living room is empty. I better get into retrospection before I go crazy. This is holy isolation, where God nor Satan can reach me, but where my mind surpasses reality.

The crickets chirp, the moon casts a faint spotlight, and the tenebrous darkness illuminates the power of my mind. At my desk with pen and paper, a Coleman lamp that flickers, and a small fire that crackles and flashes concepts, ideas, aphorisms, characters, and even beautiful places, I write the power of my mind......

men is the smartest animal,   we are born alone and alone we die   being, being is extending your arms and feeling, let the wind take you,   nature is in you   what should I write about? Something moves around the house,   the floor crackles,   things stretch, the owl hoots I miss Rose, she should be here!   What was that?

A face just peeked from upstairs,   it cannot be Rose

I need to concentrate,   what is my philosophy?   Scratch that!   In all this time not hungry   maybe   a   sip   of cognac will calm my nerves,   oh yes, soothing   more yes,

my body is a leaf yes,   ok it is time to write now!

Beauty and happiness cannot be heard from others, cannot be read in a book, and cannot be tasted   you have to live it, your being must feel it   because hours and days pass   and time will not have mercy,   regret is the greatest pain there is,   death comes and it is over   no ritual, no religion, no god, can prove of an afterlife,

this is the opportunity take your shame, your fear,   take words, deeds, laments   bury them like priceless gold, later they will make you realize the true price of happiness,   what was that?!

I peek outside but nothing is visible, wait   some shadows move, no! Need to write more!   Love?   Love is the fear of losing something, we cherish it because it makes us happy but we hate to see it make others happy   it is not pure, it is not selfless   it is all for us to validate our existence, without it we would just be, just ourselves without any regards to what others say about what they experience,   I guess what I mean is that love is the seek for validation,   we don't really need it, or do we need love? The mornings without the one that makes us full, the afternoons without a reflective conversation, when nobody calls you, nobody loves you, you do what you want... is that freedom or sadness? the pines, this cabin, my desk, the majestic woods, they are separate,   they are not an illusion but material matter that give us feelings, and then we react to those feelings

but once we die,   the material cannot just cease to exist, they have been there   the material world exists before and after our life   therefore feelings are but an illusions   perception   is knowledge   creepy footsteps, I have lots of cognac and even rum... ah, this is good… then why does it matter? If things go after we go, why worry? Life? It's just a brief opportunity to see   to feel, that's it   not much to it, music, I can see music   the fire dies, the world moves......

There is a murky fog this morning. It hovers like ghosts through the trees. The pines have a faded green hue, and a thread of whispers echoes in the cabin. My hands freeze from inside my gloves, and my body shivers rapidly, but I restart the fire. My desk is filled with papers. Useless cowshit is what this is! How could I write such things? My eyes itch. Maybe some coffee will settle my mood. The pot's bubbling resonates in the cabin, and the pleasant aroma of brewed coffee soothes my frozen nostrils. My eyes widen, and my body reheats. It is a rare pleasure to write and enjoy coffee without any distractions.

A white horse gallops out of the woods and stops in front of the cabin. It moves in circles and locks eyes with me. Strange, I should get back to writing......

What to write, what to write......

Nothing comes out! This stray horse will not destroy my peace. I step out with my shotgun and scare it away. The horse snorts several times and gives a loud squeal. It then runs off into the forest. *Ruben... Ruben... Ruben...*that voice, it's so familiar, *Ruben...* Sounds like it is coming from the wilderness. My desk awaits me, but those voices are far more attractive than pen and paper. Just a peek, that's all. Writing is more important. That voice, however, sounds like my muse...

Oh, lord! I scratch my eyes and blink several times. Sarah walks up to me, stunning, unsympathetic, and alive? Her delicate feet produce rhythmic waves of angelic chants, she strokes my face, but I can't look at her straight in the eye. My ear tickles as she whispers to me.

"Stop writing. Nobody cares." She says. This can't be her. This must be the spirit of the forest or some odd shit. I need to go back and get proper rest.

"Stop writing!" Sarah yells. I take a few steps back. She extends her arms and twitches her head. I run. My eyes roll in every direction, but my cabin is nowhere to be found. Finally, she disappears, but her sinister laughter echoes through the trees.

"Sarah, come out!" I yell, and a shadow dashes behind me.

THE BAD BLESSINGS

"Sarah, stop!" Cold sweat pours down my face.

She sounds so close, but I can't find her. A shadow shifts behind a tree. Is it Sarah, or have I lost it? I prepare to fire, but my heart beats faster, and my hands quiver incessantly. I aim at the other side of the trunk... nothing.

The fog begins to dissipate, the sun warms the ambiance and my nerves, and as I raise my head, the rays scatter across my skin. The pungent smell of damp moss and the singing birds dispel any sense of evil. Pleased by the sound of my feet cracking through the leaves, I walk back to my cabin. But then, my ears are stunned by a thunderous waterfall. I follow the sound... oh, a waterfall is a perfect place for meditation. There is a river that curves through the trees; its blue-gem sparkles draw me closer and closer. My feet step on glistening pebbles. Across the bank, an unlikely expectation, Rose stands lifeless. "Rose!" She doesn't respond. Suddenly, she breaks into a cry and sinks down to her knees. My feet plunge into the river, and the water consumes my body, but my Rose is near......

My Rose, my love, wait for me, don't go, don't cry!
I should have never left, I should have stayed with my family like
a good man   a good man, but... Rose swirls above the clear
icy water,   illusions cascade with bubbles, oh yes,
how refreshing, my pain,   my happiness,   almost   gone,
everything in my life is now on these froths of bubbles finally I
reach the bank,   perseverance has always stood by me,
but everything is blank, like the day I opened my eyes,   I made

it, I'll be there my love, it is better to have false hope than no hope at all......

7

The shitty thing is that it's painful......

A cloud of thick smoke fills the tiny garage, the stench of gasoline stings my nostrils, and each breath becomes shorter and shorter. The exit has a row of junk cars and my dress rips from the sharp rusty edges… some escape. Michael's creepy Victorian house stands to the side of the garage like a dormant giant. A specter watches me from behind those dark curtains, but nothing can be as horrible as Michael's family. They don't like me. I am perhaps too good for their son, their good son that nearly set the house on fire. Love is endurance, right?

Michael steps out of the thick smoke with oil smudges on his boiler suit. He removes his goggles, and his eyes are the only part untouched by the smoke; he smirks. I would give anything to not see him work like a slave. That smoke is like our lives, toxic and blurry. We both want wealth and success, but there are too many obstacles. We hardly kiss because we don't have time for anything but work. But he loves me. He must love me. After a two-year relationship, things should be serious. Wealth, stability, and ambition are the real illusions that hurt our relationship. Love? We really don't know the true meaning of love. At least he doesn't know it. He gives me a peck on the cheek and runs back to his house. Despite Michael's dryness, anything is possible in his arms; happiness, protection, dreams, and even escape from my strange family. Pa breaks my life; Michael breaks my sorrow.

Michael is a hardworking man. He aspires to be a professional racer and auto engineer. But tradition and religion are the gatekeepers of anything in this town. His father, Michael Miller, is the pastor of the only church, a place for boring sermons and big tithes. His mother is a devoted prude who neglects his dreams and wants him to marry a dull-witted church girl. My intentions are pure. His success is my pride, at my side, of course. Unfortunately, Amourville is not the place to raise a family and achieve our dreams. We are stranded at sea; there is not much hope. Only the hope, vague hope, that we both stop staring at each other and look in the same direction. One day…

He rushes out of his house and hands me a cup of water. A sense of disgust overtakes me, but a few drops soothe my smoked-filled throat.

"Epic fail!" I choke on the water.

"No, why?" He wipes the water from his mouth.

"Because you have been working on this car forever."

"It will run. I just need a little bit more time and…."

"Money…" I cut him off. "The one thing we don't have."

THE BAD BLESSINGS

"Don't start; you sound like my parents."

"When are we moving out, Michael? We need to start our lives."

Michael taps his boiler suit… "My ring!" He rushes back to the garage. He always avoids this conversation.

Our promise ring sparkles in his hand. Perhaps he does care about us, even in the most minor details. But he is not expressive, a loveless 19-year-old soul, cold and bitter; how will I put up with him?

He sits on his porch and writes on a small notepad. Not those interminable budgets again! Save for this, save for that…He writes budgets and budgets yet still has no money. His parents don't give him much money, or perhaps the church offerings are insufficient to fulfill his ambitions. Michael does not have a stable job. He has a few customers, but there are many other qualified mechanics. Church people bring him food and offerings. He feels set for life, but how can we progress like this? It is always about his cars, money, and plans. What about me? Our most dreaded subject is marriage; the word alone makes him cringe. Kids, a house, marriage, everything is too soon for him except cars and money.

Michael has no future except with me by his side. His parents want him to be the next pastor. He no longer attends school to be an excellent servant to Jehovah, but he does not have an inch of God's love, nor can he be a professional racer in this town. All he can ever be is a lonely mechanic, that's all—

if he is any good. He wants to please his parents and pursue his dreams. My love and my heart are just casualties. But that is what he thinks; this painful situation will change. I will make my family proud, even if I must kill, even if I must lie. My dreams will be fulfilled, and Rose will look up to me! Fuck hope, fuck destiny. I control my future, and today Michael and I will look in the same direction, even if we fail.

He stops his notes and pulls out a hip flask.......

He still drinks?!   Why?!   Why can't he just stop!
Stop!   A failure and a drunk!   No but, he is the
love of my life   that butt chin, those blue eyes, that wavy black
hair   his skin like a god   Rose's
guy is ugly!   But this guy!   Why does he drink,   why
can't he listen to me   I am the only person that truly loves him
please my love stop   then we won't be able to have kids   I will
convince him   I will manipulate him   he loves me
he knows I am right......

"Love, why are you drinking again?"

"Stop judging me. I don't do it every day and I am home, not out with friends."

"Then how will we ever have a family like this?"

"Ah crap! Really, here we go again! The same thing over and over again."

He gets up and socks the old porch column.

"You spend your money on alcohol and expect to get rich? How the hell..."

"Ok, Kashmir, stop. You don't understand what I am going through!"

"Michael, please stop drinking. Otherwise, we will never get out of this situation."

"We still won't get out. You have nothing."

"At least I don't live off the church money."

Michael shuts his eyes and taps his head.

"Then we can't be together. Our dreams are just talk, that's it. Talk and shit." He says.

> ...... *Just talk   shit   I suffer with Pa,*
> *Ma pressures me to get married and stupid Rose always judging me   why*
> *is her life so easy   why does Pa love her so much   1   am*
> *not losing him,   he loves me   but he just needs support*
> *   he needs to know that I am his right hand   he needs*
> *to know I will not leave him   oh crap with what money...*
> *Pa why do you hate me?!   I can make you proud, I*
> *can... that's right   Pa, must give me   the family inheritance,*
> *but it belongs to that bitch Rose!   No!*
> *She does not deserve it,   I deserve it,   I am the pride of the family,*
> *   Rose is a selfish, useless person   but   that*
> *wealth will solve all our problems, make things the way we want them, I*
> *have to get it , I must somehow, I think I know... church, God,*

whatever… that's all crap…   money, greed, ambition are all bad
blessings,   my bad blessings   we will be rich, and he will race cars
and I will race his heart and mind……

"In-he-ri-tan-ce…" I whisper.

"What did you say?" He says.

Money is his weakness. I can't blame him. If my plan can grant us eternal happiness, then so be it; money is the bait. Money can buy happiness.

"If I convince my father to give me the inheritance, we can use the money to fulfill our dreams far from here."

He thinks for a moment… Michael then burst into laughter. But I know Rose's love can be used against Pa. I can do it.

"You are crazy, just crazy. Get a job." He says.

"If you love me, shut up and trust my plan."

He shrugs and sits next to me. His capricious whistle does not anger me anymore, but I take a deep breath to prepare myself for this moment.

"I will get rid of Rose, don't ask me how but I can do it. My family is falling apart, and Pa will have no choice but to give me the inheritance. I will not fail.…"

"Kashmir, if you fail, this relationship is over. I can't stop for anybody, I love you, but I have goals."

"Trust me, just this once, my love."

I wipe the sweat from his face, and he strokes my head. His stroke is gentle yet forced. Why even try to kiss him? All he has in his head is money. But my plan is the greatest show of love, love will prevail.

My love and future are at stake. I cannot fail. Others should suffer, not me. Why do others get things handed to them? Why is love hard? Why does love need money? Something is always missing in my life, and it torments me… but my life will change. If I cannot have Michael, then nobody will have Michael's love.

This old mirror is more than a reflection. It is my emergence from suffering. A thin crack slices my smile in half, but it shines despite imperfection. I am strong, there is power inside me, and my family will feel it. Pa and Rose will regret their hate. Rose walks in with a sullen expression and tosses herself in bed. Perfect opportunity: it must be Joseph again. This family is too small for both of us, but tonight only one will remain.

"I am meeting some friends at *Comparis*. Let's go!" I say.

Rose whimpers into her pillow, then she lifts her bloodshot eyes.

"Ever since when do you invite me out?"

"Michael and I broke up, and I need…I need you, sister, please. Like when Pa took us when we were little…."

"I remember. Whatever happened to those family days…."

Rose moves next to me and strokes my face. "What is happening with our family?" She says in a low tone.

"Hardships, every family has a dark side. But we can fix it, sister…." I rub my face against her repugnant hands.

"We have been focusing too much on love when we should focus on our family. We should heal first before we find true love. Let's make Ma and Pa proud…." I whisper in her ear.

Ma steps into the room. She gesticulates a prayer and strokes our faces.

"What are you two ladies up to?"

"Rose and I are about to head out for sister time…r-i-g-h-t?"

Rose clears her throat. She exchanges glances between Ma and I. She is not a people pleaser, but Ma's jubilant smile convinces her.

"I wanted to rest and not see the world, but sure, relive our childhood days and spend time with my little sister." Rose says.

THE BAD BLESSINGS

"¡Ay! ¡*Gracias a Dios*! My little girls. You better get going before it gets late. Don't forget your Pa's blessing."

Rose rushes into the bathroom.......

That's right, spend time with your sister, even if it is the last time   hell no! You don't know what's coming up Rose   your life is going to change   Kashmir All for me and my Michael   what we have is true love,   what girl would go as far as manipulation just to see him happy!   ME! ONLY ME!   Take your time Rose, you must dress for the occasion   Michael in his dream car, a house full of kids and trophies, and I the woman, the pride,   and above all a happy mother! I can taste it, this plan is working......

Pa drinks coffee in the living room. He gives Rose a kiss on the forehead but only sneers at me.

"You look out for your sister, Kashmir." Pa says.

Stupid old man, I am not my sister's keeper. Pa is old or perhaps too sensitive. That's why Rose gets away with things I wouldn't be allowed to, like going out at night. Rose puts her arm around me and kisses my head. Pa smiles at Rose and rolls his eyes at me. Fine, I'll be glad to look out for my sister. You will regret this Pa, along with all those times you tormented me. Soon I'll be free, and you will give me the thing that I yearn for every day, your love...

The yeasty aroma of freshly baked bread stirs my stomach like a whirlpool and brings back memories of my happy family… Pa's lovelier days. Rose orders the pizza, like always. The tiny booths contain the colors of the Italian flag– red, white, and green. They are neatly arranged along a red brick wall, with just enough space to move around. Behind the cozy dining area, there is an impressive facade of a balcony. The owner says it symbolizes his parents first love encounter back in Italy. How romantic, but Michael would make many excuses not to see me if I had a balcony. Love is complicated, but tonight the tables will turn.

We sit near an oven, and the heat waves warm our stiff cold skin. Rose hates small talk, but it's not the right time to strike. Meanwhile, my eyes scroll at the photos of Italian American immigrants and Roman history. These photos are lovely. Perhaps one day I will visit Italy when I am wealthy with Michael at my side. A painting of Venus goddess of love, smiles at me. Give me your blessing because everything is in the name of love, stability, and sex.

"I am happy little sister. You are coping well from your heartbreak." Rose says.

"I do have help."

"From whom? Your friends?"

"Maybe. Thank you for coming sister."

"I still feel as if we are not sisters. Something is a bit off, don't you think?"

What a suspicious little bitch. This plan is more complex than I thought...I better change this face, but how do I strike? When? Patience, breathe and do everything with love.

"What is really going on, Kashmir?"

The pizza arrives, but her stupid question blunts my hunger and peace. Rose is secretive and cunning. She knows how to get to people but gets angry when they poke her in the wrong spots. Joseph must be troubling her; the perfect place to start.

"Why did you break up with Joseph?"

She sets down her glass of seltzer, and frowns.

"It just did not work out...."

"But why, he was an amazing guy, your high school sweetheart, the man that Ma and Pa expect you to...."

"Kashmir! I don't want to talk about it, ok...."

"Ok... sorry... just trying to be nice...."

"I don't ask you the details about Michael."

"You never really loved Joseph, just tell me that... sister."

Rose gives me a sullen stare, then an awkward silence permeates the table; the only sound comes from the nearby murmurs.

"Don't you ever judge me." Rose says.

"My dear sister, let's take the first step toward happiness. Take off your blindfold."

"Michael was a fuck boy. He never loved you. I bet he cheated on you."

......bitch really?   No! she lies   I   can't let her win   My Michael, would you cheat on me?
        I have seen him flirt a couple times but... she can't win,   but it seems to be working   the more mad she gets, the less she thinks   her mind is cloudy while mine is fresh   this is my green light......

Rose is about to burst, and she will lose her temper. Now is the time to leave.

"Kashmir!"

She tries to call me back. Fuck her. I walk back to the car.

Rose knocks on the window. She has some empathy, as fake as the restaurant façade. Cold-hearted, hypocritical, and unwilling to say sorry, it's a horror we are sisters. My blood boils to hear her nonsense. People turn to look at us. It is no use to have her yell outside. Rose steps into the car. I light up a bud and take a resounding hit. My coughs propel a cloud of smoke. She stares at my bud, baffled. This is the finest weed from the valley; her words can't hurt me. Nature is on my side...

"Pain is the only thing we have in common. I want to see us happy, but I fail; I am lonely, and I want all these bad things to stop... I can't... I..." The words parch in my throat.

She crosses her arms and looks away. I take another hit and hand her the bud, but she looks at me with disdain.

"Please, sister! Don't tell anyone my misery, especially Pa. He is old. I don't want to shame him."

Rose rolls her eyes between the bud and my sullen face. Then, after a moment, she smirks and takes it out of my hands.

"I feel you, little sister. Sorry for being mean...." She says.

She breaks into a whimper, and her hand shivers as she places the bud in her mouth. She better not drop it...hypocritical tears. Rose can't even feel pain. But it is working; she is weak. Rose then wipes her tears and takes a good hit......

Perfect, let nature take its course   *I will be fine... hahaha!   The smoke stayed in my mouth, this plan is fun, she thinks I am high   let her be high as hell just hang on my love, soon the inheritance will be mine   another hit or two and she will regret the day she was born   hit number two is a little longer damn she is good, she loves this   I never knew this side of her! moments later, she is more relaxed and smiley, how nice to see my sister happy   I am feeling a little   a little   high?   but I am ok oh time does not fly, it plods......*

"Kashmir. Don't tell anyone, ok." She slurs and gives me the bud.

"It's ok. We are sisters." I say.

She snatches the joint from my mouth and gives it another good blow.

"I don't like guys. I like girls... ok."

"Oh no...Pa will be mad...."

"He cannot know. Promise you won't tell. Promise me, sweet little sister."

"Give me your birthright to the family inheritance...." I whisper in her ear.

Rose stares out the window, dazed and silent. She then turns to look at me with bloodshot eyes and frowns.

"I can't, you know...   that, that I think is mine, I know is mine."

"Then Pa will know the truth, sweet sister. Honor comes first. That is what Pa taught us."

Rose moves her head sideways and then finishes the last tip of the bud. She then fumbles with her purse until I open it for her. Rose stares at the purse, dumbfounded, and then yells at it. She has a good high. What a sad show, my dear big sister, but it's funny.

"Ok, what do you really want? Please elaborate so I can go home!" Rose says.

She leans on the window, and her eyes twitch.

"Give me your birthright to the Rendar inheritance, and I promise Pa will not know you like girls. We love Pa, and we must keep him alive."

Rose nods incessantly and grips my hair. Almost there, I just need to hear those words…

"You can have it, sweet little sister."

"Text it to me please because I might forget. Remember, it is all for Pa."

Rose struggles with her phone. She looks at me and drops her mouth. I grab her hands and hold the phone to her face.

"Text me this: I give you my inheritance and birthright sister. Please don't tell Pa I am a lesbian."

She slurs the words and types the message, letter by letter. An eternity later, my phone vibrates… When angels fail, demons help…

My muscles tense, and my feet tickle. Oh shit, Grams rubs my feet. I feel a little groggy with flashes from last night.

"Where is Rose?" I say.

Grams points to the door. My phone is under my pillow with a little bit of battery. I scroll through the text messages, and there it is, my sister's service to the family and my greatest accomplishment. Grams scowls at my chuckles and walks towards the door.

"My sweet little girl, you are showering with a faucet of flames."

"What day is it, Grams?"

She stares at me for a moment and then looks around the room. She then taps her head and pulls out a wrinkled paper filled with notes.

"Um, what did you say?" She asks.

"Have you had coffee?"

She nods and walks out of the room. Poor Grams, every day she gets older and older. I'll send her to a retirement home, where she can die in peace and take a weight off our shoulders. My palms itch…riches await me. I can't contain this joy after years of sorrow. Voices shout from the kitchen… this must be good.

Rose steps into her car and accelerates out the driveway. I move to the living room, where Pa sips his coffee. He is a calf, waiting for the predator.

"Father, we must talk."

"I don't have money. Get a job like your sister."

I go on my knees and stroke his callous hands.

"Rose gave up her birthright and inheritance to me...."

Pa chokes on his coffee, and stares at me, baffled. I show him her text message. His hand shivers, his eyes widen, and after a silent moment, he shuts his teary eyes.

"Rose betrayed us, but I am here to make you proud!"

Pa digs his hand into my hair and tightens his grip.

"You planned this, didn't you?"

"No, she texted me don't you see! It was her secret. She fooled us!"

Pa throws me against the couch. He grunts and destroys everything in his path. Glass shatters, and coffee spills all over the kitchen.

"That inheritance will never be yours, never! No matter what happens!"

He prepares to punch me.

"Give me the inheritance, or Rose will hate you for the rest of your miserable life...."

"Stupid little girl, you think I believe you?!"

He grabs my arm and squeezes it with all his rage.

"Stay away from Rose, or I will kill you!"

His warm saliva burns my face, but I push him away. My arm hurts, but I am strong.

"Then swear you will give me the inheritance she gave up. If not, I will report you to the police."

Pa takes a few steps away from me. He then takes a seat and breathes rapidly.

"What the hell do you know about the police?"

"It is in the newspapers. Some Sarah lady used to call the store when Ma was not there. I just never said anything because I did not care. But I know you killed her; the detectives came by the other day. You are a sick man, sick, sick. My big sister will be repulsed by you…."

"If you say something, I'll kill you."

"Give me what I want, or Rose finds out her daddy is a murderer."

He shuts his eyes and tightens his teeth. Pa can't swallow his pride, just like Rose.

"Swear to me!" I shout.

A deafening silence permeates the kitchen. He stares at the floor, absent-minded.

"The inheritance is…y-o-u-r-s… I swear…" His voice cracks.

"How do I know you are not lying…father?"

"Meet me at the notary at 1pm…you win, just stay away from Rose, or I will kill you."

Damn, this feels so good. I walk out of the house like an empress, unstoppable and everlasting. Life is full of injustices, but sometimes intelligence means being a little evil. I have nothing to lose. I love myself and my Michael. But mostly myself…

It is 1:45pm, and Pa does not show up. Pa is fooling me. Asshole, how could he? What will I tell Michael? Oh, my God… fuck my life, how can he do this? How can an old fool outsmart me? My life is over…

Epic failure… Forgive me my love. You are free to go and fulfill your dreams. What does hope bring? Shadows, thoughts, a painful body, reality? Then comes more grief, and then sorrow feeds me hope again. Hope hurts me but hope never ends. It is my bad blessing. Perhaps suicide is much easier than living.

My mouth turns salty, and acid swirls up my throat. I place my face in the toilet, but nothing comes out. What is wrong with me? I feel dizzy. A warm drip oozes out my vagina. Spotting? It can't be my period. A sudden pang pulls me from inside!......

What is wrong with me? What is this nasty pressure?

I thought I was a bad bitch but now I have nothing,   my own father played   me,   my own sister played me and soon my boyfriend will stop loving me   ok   why does my stomach hurt fuck I can't go   throw up… I can't throw up   Wait, am I pregnant,   Michael always uses a condom,   and he does not want kids   what will I tell him now   I don't want to live anymore, why does all this matter, I can't be rich   I can't please my boyfriend, and I failed him   if I am pregnant

I am going to abort, sorry,   or yeah just kill myself, it is easier to kill myself   than to ever live a life where nobody likes me or where I just can't get everything I want!   What is this?   A pregnancy test? This shit is not mine; I swear but it has been here it's…   Rose!   a positive!   How can this be? What a little whore   Mom must know, if I did not get what I want, then Rose will suffer too……

Rose storms into the bathroom, pale and out of breath. I drop the test stick and rush to my bed. Rose takes a deep breath and walks over to the window, stony-faced and silent. My only desire is to kill her. Rose whimpers… what a hypocrite.

"You can have the family inheritance Kashmir."

"So, he did give it to you?"

"Yes, but I own up to my mistakes."

She turns to me, completely serious, but I don't believe her.

"Are you doing this because now I know you are pregnant?" I say.

"No, because I know that without this, you are nobody. I don't need an inheritance to care for my family. I make my own destiny."

Her fake generosity is just too coincidental. How can she give up a valuable inheritance out of loyalty to a murderer, a liar? She needs that inheritance to sustain the family. There must be more to her generosity, although she seems hurt… Rose shows me a folder full of documents.

"This is what you want, but you can only have it under one condition."

I knew it, there is something in it for her, cunning bitch…

"You can never come back to this house nor speak to Ma and Grams. We don't need anything from you, do you understand?"……

My mother, my dear sweet mother, how cruel, how can I not see her again   I shouldn't agree   why is she so cruel   but Michael, now I can see him happy, we will have everything we dreamed of   but mother will cry   I can't choose   mother always dreamed of seeing me with a big family and kids   she won't see it but she will know that her little girl made her proud not like this dumb lesbian, Sorry mother, but I want my own life,   no matter what Rose says, I will return to see you   one day you will understand my decision   Why can't I have everything   things are in the world for a reason   and I must be free to take what makes me happy, right… yet I have the things that make me sad, those are always available   well lesson learned, I can't have everything, I am not free to choose how I will get my wishes, if this is it then, so be it, I choose happiness, however it comes……

"I understand, our ties end here." I say.

Rose nods and hands me the documents.

"We will go to a notary in the big city to transfer everything to your name."

"Why?"

"Because the notary in this town will destroy your weak self-esteem."

Her eyes are glossy. Poor thing, she is poor and condemned to care for two old ladies. I even want to cry for her. But she deserves pain, and I am happy to see her die from the inside.

"I am sorry, sister. It hurts me to see you like this. Please don't take revenge. I did it all for our family." I say.

"My revenge is to know you will suffer for everything. One day you will regret it." Rose says.

A little angel flies into the room. His yellow wings are lovely. At last, an angel instead of that creepy shadow guy, how wonderful! The angel leaves a trail of stardust and a sweet smell of lilies. I try to catch him, but he is swift. His heartening giggle gives me tears of joy. My children will giggle too. I can hear them. The angel turns to Rose, but she digs her face into the pillow and cries. The poor thing frowns and cries next to her. *Kashmir… Kashmir… Kashmir*, the angel whispers my name. He takes my hand and pulls me towards the door. The angel exerts a great force to lift us into the air. My wings sprout and we fly into the heavens. But then the sun melts my wings like drops of molasses and the sky turns red. The little angel turns to stone and crumbles into the ground. I crash land on a red ocean, the water boils. My skin melts, but a handsome stranger offers me his hand. He pulls me out, and I am back in the room with Rose. The more I see the world, the more I realize that it takes imagination to be happy. Reality is just overrated.

Michael is not in the garage. He does not answer my calls or texts. These spasms are like a rock that rolls and rips my intestines; it hurts badly! But this glorious moment is priceless, the perfect cure for my pain. Michael's mother waters her withered garden. She clashes eyes with me but pretends not to notice.

"Is Michael home, Mrs. Miller? I can't find him."

She takes off her gloves and wipes the sweat from her sunburned skin. A faint smile covers her wrinkled face, and she walks to the porch without saying a word. She is a strange woman.

"My dear, dear, Kashmir, I could not recognize you. I thought you were little Ms. Wordsworth."

My blood boils. Small talk and stupidity tick me off so much.

"Where is your son?!"

A luxurious Cadillac pulls up the driveway. It is Sondra Wordsworth, the major's daughter. Michael steps out of the house, and his mother looks down with a smirk. His elegant suit and radiant countenance accelerate my heartbeat, and this awkward triangle turns my leg into noodles.

"I am sorry, Kashmir. Days passed, and you never called back. I was going to tell you." He says.

Tears blur the sight of his awfully perfect face. Reality torments me again; imagination is a farce, and hope is an illusion.

"But I got the inheritance!"

"Kashmir, I am not ready for a serious relationship. I want to work for myself."

"Son of a bitch. You never loved me. Rose was right…."

Sondra steps out of the truck and crosses her arms. My rage pushes me to pull her ugly hair, but Michael snatches my arm.

"Let go of me, asshole!"

Michael shoves me away. They look so lovely together, a whore and an asshole. I want to rip her pretty face. If I can't have him, nobody can't...what good will that do? Revenge? I have wealth and property. I can have any man in the world. I hate him, and I love him; how is this possible? I don't know, I require too much, perhaps there is a perfect someone out there for me... bullshit, I love myself.

"Kashmir, we need to talk later when you are calm."

"I never want to see you again. I wish you the best."

Sondra throws a fit, and Michael struggles to calm her. His mother wobbles on the porch with a smile, the most horrendous smile I have ever seen. Sick old fart. I hope she dies soon. I hope she smiles when Sondra fucks all the boys from church. Michael shoves Sondra into the truck. He then runs after me.

I shut my door and start the car. He bangs on the window... Rose's voice bounces in my head. My back wheels disperse a cloud of dust that dissolves all the love in my heart, a dust cloud that buries my sweet past. It hurts to get lost in the heart of a man, to kiss the ground he walks on, and to hope...but much worse is to forget that I exist, that I must seek my own happiness, and the less hope, the less disappointment...

My hands are sweaty, and my body cringes from the blast of the air conditioner. The smell of disinfectant and the blinding white walls spin my head. Those diagrams of the reproductive system, posters advocating condoms, advocating adoption, and anti-abortion slogans make me nauseous. I hate doctor visits. After an eternal minute, the doctor steps in with a serious expression. He opens the file and clears his throat several times. He rolls his eyes up.

"The results show you have two large tumors in your ovaries. We need to operate immediately."

"Oh, God, well then, yes. So, is that what this pain is all about?"

"Yes, in all likelihood."

He sits on his chair and gasps, "I must warn you that if we remove the tumors, the ovaries will be too damaged. We will remove them, and you will not be able to have kids. You will start menopause…."

A saber rips through my chest. Today, God is truly dead. Everything I want is grains of sand that crumble out of my hands. Who am I? What am I? I age without aging. I want kids, kids are the joy of my life, but now, what will I have now? Pain? It is time to have hope, that is it, what else… oh my children! But hope… hope brings me sorrow, again… There is only one thing I dread: not being worthy of my suffering.

There comes Ron, he is Brazilian and so exotic. Ron is smoother and works me up very well. Stephen is too rough and needs pills; I cannot deal with that. Confident men make me feel like a younger woman. Ron is handsome, lovely, and cares for minor details. He does not miss a holiday and always spends time with me. We call my house our palace, and we do it at least once in each of the five rooms. Hard work and suffering pay off. I love Ron, but the age difference may separate us. I am 40, and he can easily find a girl at least 10 years younger than him. But why is he with me? I can't have kids, and he knows it. Perhaps he cheats on me, but his experience in bed destroys any of my doubts, or at least satisfies my cravings for pleasure, which really matters to me.

Love in the big city is impressive, diverse, and free. Deep empty loneliness overcomes me when he is away on his business trips. I don't need money; the lands are sold, and my past boyfriends are still on good terms. I only work as a teaching assistant to be around people and enjoy meaningful conversations. I love my life, I love Ron, and I love my accomplishments. But loneliness eats me, suicide still roams my mind, yet pleasure overpowers me. Pleasure might get old one of these days, perhaps older than me. The night is so beautiful, Ron must be on his way, and as soon as he takes me in his arms, we will contemplate the beauty of the stars. Soon one of those little stars will be dust, and it won't shine. That's how our love is, shiny like a star but dusty as rotten bones, but why worry? Life is too short, and it might end one of these days…

8

Ma stumbles into an array of banker boxes in my room. We will move to the big city. There is nothing but sorrow in this house, aside from other strange things. Ma wants me to stay in Amourville. It will take time until she realizes that we don't need men, if she ever realizes her potential. It is best to put the past behind, even if the past is what makes… us. Ma sits at the edge of my bed and rolls her eyes all over the tiny pink room. She then puts her head down and whispers to herself… *How will we eat?* … over and over. After Pa's scandal, customers don't come as often. Kashmir plans to sell the property and our acres of land, including the store. Ma claims that Kashmir sends money here and there, but I doubt that will last forever. Kashmir is greedy.

My goal is to move to the big city and start law school. I am perfectly capable of being a mother and a student. Life hurts, but that does not mean it is full of pain. Anything bad can bring good too. Ma wants to help me raise the child. She gladly accepts my queerness. Amourville is the worst place to raise a child; even the gas is too expensive for commuting. Our future is in the big city, and we can't let fear stop us. Fear is not one of my attributes. To ease her uncertainty, we search for the big city streets on Google Images… we see the nightlife, women with women, men with women, true love, unity, and modernity. Ma giggles, but her face shows confusion. She comes across a couple expressing their love over the enchanting city lights. She whispers… *Harry* and looks out the window, love-struck. Even Amourville cannot suck the romance out of her. Ma then gazes at my mess. I did not realize the amount of clothes I had in this room. She pulls out a little painting. A rainbow emerges from a girl's heart. She runs her fingers through the canvas. Perhaps she wants reassurance that things will be better, like in the old days……

> *I am here, everything that is here is all that exists*
> *all else not in front of my eyes does not exist,   thoughts, illusions,*
> *the past, people, the dead   reality is our interpretation, that's all but I*
> *guess we think too much,   just too much of what is not there*
> *but how can mother understand that?   We need*
> *to move   life is not life here   but she is afraid*
> *afraid of what?   I don't even know   I   don't*
> *even know how I can convince her, how can father have caused so much*
> *damage,   how?   Why?   Kashmir   really?*
> *How could you?,   to your own family… I only   wish   her   the   best*
> *because Ma and Grams need it   I am   hungry,   too much   packing,*
> *maybe a snack   Ma whimpers   she is like a little dumb girl,*
> *but I love that little dumb girl……*

I hug Ma and kiss her forehead.

"We will always be together, despite the loss of the inheritance. My success will be your pride."

Ma smiles and wipes her tears; she agrees to pack tomorrow. It is Saturday night, our traditional movie night.

The sweet aroma of ghee tickles my nose as Ma's popcorn crackles. Ma then serves popcorn and coffee, a nostalgic movie night staple. Grams sleeps in her room because she likes to keep to herself. Our small living room feels big because the family is smaller, but our love remains big. Ma loves romantic comedies. Her eyes glisten when the lovers meet and when they stay together. Pa can't judge her anymore. She is a hopeless romantic, but Ma is free and happy. A man is not necessary to feel happy; perhaps she will realize it soon. But Laura… Where is she? Does she think of me? The other side of the sofa is cold. My hand stretches to seek Laura's warmth, but there is only the old, wrinkled leather of the couch. Ma understands me. She knows that love is love, but love is not for me. Time will erase the remorse in my heart. Time can't, however, destroy the memories of the past. How do I know it is me without my past? Laura will be in me forever…

Ma breaks into tears at the end of this movie. Hopefully, this poor woman sleeps with someone she loves before death.

"Did you love father?" I say.

"I thought I did… no, maybe not.…" Ma wipes her eyes.

Despite Pa's actions, I am who I am because of him. Because of him, I am not like Ma; I can live without the need for love… because of him, I am here with what's left of my family.

It's that thing again! … That shadow walks into the kitchen, and Ma turns to me with panic-stricken eyes. A dead silence fills the living room; the only sound comes from the movie soundtrack.

"Did you see that?" I ask.

Ma nods. A ghastly whisper calls my name…

Rose… Rose…Rose…

"Who is that?" I rush to the kitchen.

"Where are you going?" Ma's voice fades away…

Rose… Rose… the creepy whisper echoes.

My hand fumbles in the dark for the kitchen light. Those two red eyes move towards me and reveal the head of a pale horse. Worms crawl out of its mouth, its brittle mane grows incessantly, and blood bursts out of its eyes. My heart races, and my legs tremble. The horse reveals its scrawny short body. It tries to reach me with its pale wiggly fingers, but my body is lost in this pitch darkness. A baby cries, the echo rips my ears, and my name sounds again. *Rose…* that's Pa's voice! My Pa is here! The child's cry overrides his voice. A pendulum clock appears… time runs counterclockwise as the dials melt. The horse's body regenerates, its skin shines, and the mane becomes healthy. A woman's happy laughter fades in… Laura runs behind the horse trying to reach me. My body falls into an abyss, and her body melts into blood… "Mother!" I yell.

The lights turn on, and my weak body drops into Ma's arms. She battles to put me in a chair, as my eyes gaze around the kitchen, I realize it was not a dream.......

That was father,   and my Laura
and the little horse   who is that?
That can't be a dream, I was there   mother
oh, I can feel her, it is   over   but the baby, what about
the baby!?......

Ma drags me to the sofa, the living room spins, and my mouth is dry. A blurry shadow walks into the living room.

"Is the child coming?" The voice says.

I squint, and after a moment, my vision clears up. It is Grams with her giant glasses.

"The child?" Ma says.

"No, I don't think so." I reply.

Grams sits next to me and rubs my belly. Mother hands me water with sugar, an old superstition to relieve a shock.

"I am okay, just in shock...but I am okay...."

"This is very familiar. I saw it once." Grams says.

We look at her with profound confusion.

"Saw what, mother?" Ma asks.

"What did you see, dear?" Grams asks.

"It was very dark, like a, uh… dark hole, I don't know. Then a nasty horse with a baby's body, crying and crying. It was like dancing with his hands, and then I heard Pa's voice and then…." Grams interrupts me…

"How was it dancing?"

"I think… kind of like, like African ladies dancing and jumping."

Grams stares at me, absentminded. She then lays back and taps her head several times.

"What is it, mother?" Ma asks.

Grams looks me in the eye.

"You have a curse, my child. Someone wants to make you suffer."

Ma's face turns purple. My body cringes, and my hair rises.

"I don't believe in any of that." I say.

"That baby could be your child. It cries for your help. I am not sure about the horse, but your child will die if you don't break this curse."

"Did you see anything else?" Ma asks.

"No, just… a clock going counter to time and… and… I can't remember…."

"Time is against you. You must break the curse to protect your child. That dancing, maybe that was a ritual, but Ruben's voice, oh, it means darkness will come if you don't break the curse…we will die."

"Oh, my almighty God, deliver us from evil!" Ma pleads.

Gram's words stir a bit of fear within me. Her sister was a *santera*, the term for witches in Cuba, and I think in Nicaragua too. She began to practice Santeria after her husband left her with six kids. But who wants to curse me? I don't believe in that shit.

"Death surrounds you! My sister would know how to break this curse. Voices forced her man to kill his lover and hang himself. But I am not sure in your case." Grams says.

Ma pulls me to pray on our knees, but prayer is selfish and useless. This can't be a curse. We are just afraid of change. It can also be hormones, although that shadow man appears in my room too often. Could Grams be right?

No! I don't believe in God or in superstition. I believe in what my eyes can see. My body burns from the inside. It must be hormones, nothing else.

Ma prays to an impersonal being, a social construct that suppresses women. I detach my hands, and Ma's mouth drops.

"If God is love, then why does he only accept some loves? Love is love, right? Or only his love?" I say.

We love what we can see and touch. So, if our reason is wrong, then we are not the creation of a perfect being. So then, God is man's mistake. That's my easiest explanation and the right one.

Ma begs and begs for forgiveness. Grams strokes my head.

"She can pray all she wants, but it won't work. God left us long ago, but you are your own salvation." Grams kisses my forehead… "but of course, to get to God, you must fight the devil, and what bigger devil than your head…." She chuckles.

"Grandmother, what must I do?"

"The answer is inside you. Remember I told you that you are our only hope…."

"What if it is not a curse?"

"Then God help us… if he does exist." She shrugs.

God this, God that… but perhaps this has something to do with Pa's affair… Something stirs in my gut. Pa's words resonate in my head. Who would curse me, and how do I break this shit? I don't know, I need rest.

"Just think of your child, that's all…." Grams says. She returns to her room.

I can't bring my child into this dysfunctional environment. We need to leave this eerie house now!

Ma finishes her long prayer. She begs me to visit pastor Miller for a blessing, that hypocrite, that thief! She wants me to have faith, but I can't have faith in something I can't see. Trust? Trust must be earned... Prayer and prayer, yet our lives are forsaken. Enough thoughts, my vision blurs again. I'll go to church just to shut this lady up. At church, I'll take time off from being what I really am, a lesbian. It is a burden to be myself, but a break sounds nice because I don't know who I am anymore. A woman? A mother? A curse?... Perhaps I am nothing... Must I be something?

The nave is cold and tenebrous. A stench of mildew circulates the pews, and the mosaic windows cast a ray of colors over the gloomy transept. My eyes gaze up at the colossal walls, then they stare at the crucifix... my spine tingles. The seats have scattered old hymn books written by Charles Wesley, some guy who adapted hymns from drinking songs. Bad things are easier to learn than good things; it is human nature. Ma grabs my frozen hand. Her anxiety inspires no trust in this God.

Michael Miller, a skinny old man with thin white hair, porcelain skin, and bright blue eyes, limps into the hall. Miller sits two stalls away from us. He crosses his legs and arms, and his elegant suit adds an aura of hypocrisy and mistrust. Ma's plea seems to be a broken record to his ears, but her final words put a smirk on his face.

"Can you pray for us?"

He fixes his suit and clears his throat.

"I can pray for you, but it won't suffice." He says.

Ma rubs her eyes, "Isn't God more powerful than the devil?"

"Yes, but the lord helps those who serve him...." He scans me from head to toe.

"A bit selfish, isn't he?" I ask.

"Even God demands something in return." He replies.

"Please, pastor, we need your help."

"One prayer is but vain hope. Several prayers might work, but I will need a donation for travel and time off other duties."

Miller's words are poisonous darts. He lives off people's tithes, but Ma insists on prayer, even if we don't have money. He reaches for Ma's hand and tries to touch mine. I pull my hand away and sneer, but Ma nudges me. He barely touches my fingers. Pastor Miller performs a redundant prayer; it sounds scripted rather than out of piety. These are the most infuriating minutes of my life.

"Your former lover was here, asking for prayer too. He even joined the church."

"I don't have a lover. I am a respectful woman, Pastor." Ma says.

Ma asserts her respect for the first time. What an ass, criticizes after speaking to God. Miller crosses his arms and stares at her with contempt.

"Please don't say that again, pastor, or I won't be back." She says.

Ma pulls out a stack of bills from her purse. This is not devotion, it is fanaticism, a robbery. Where is this money from? Is that all we have left to eat?

"I am so sorry, sister… God sees everything. God is love."

She hands him the bills, "I'll get you the rest tomorrow, pastor." He smirks and gives them a quick count.

"I encourage you and your husband to attend church, not for me but for God's protection." He tells me.

"I don't have a husband. I am a lesbian."

He blinks several times, and his face turns pale, then a shade of purple. Mother's mouth drops, and a screaming silence spreads in the hall.

"Upon an hour before the fall, God thought that Satan was beautiful… You can still repent. Otherwise, these prayers are worthless…."

"What? No, Pastor!" Ma pleads.

He buttons his suit and limps away. Ma goes down on her knees and whimpers.

"Hypocrite! Thief! Son of a bitch!" I yell.

Ma gets up and pulls me away, but I purge everything I genuinely feel about his hypocrisy.......

Ah! My stomach!   The baby!   It is coming, it is time breathe... breathe... breathe... Ahhh!   Ahhh!!   A powerful pang pulls me down from the hips! A giant smashes my back with all its anger!   Breathe... breathe... oh take me, mother take me!   My body splits in half,   my legs are noodles   my child,   but what if grandmother is right... the curse......

A blurry shape stands next to me, everything spins, and voices echo. My body floats. I can't even move it. The pungent odor of antiseptic burns my nose, but with each breath, my vision clears up. It's Ma! She gives me a faint smile, and Grams sits with the Rambler at the end of the room.

"It's a boy." Ma points to a crib at the edge of my bed.

My son sleeps like an angel wrapped in white clouds. Unfortunately, my beautiful son is here to suffer. I did not want to be a teenage mom, but I vow to be a good mother, even if it costs my life.... It is for my family and my honor.

"I want to hold him."

"No! No! The curse will spread. We need potions, dances, amulets, and...."

"Be quiet, mother!"

Ma brings the child into my trembling arms.

"Be careful. Hold his head." Ma says.

He is warm and delicate, a true blessing and the Rendar pride. Am I ready for this responsibility? Yes... I think...

"Moses! His name is Moses!" Grams says.

Ma and I exchange glances. "He will bring us happiness and save us from the past." Grams says.

"Glory be to thee, Lord Jehovah!" Ma says.

Ruben is no longer my choice for a boy's name. That name carries sorrow and betrayal. My son will be a better person, and he will not have any ties to the family's dark past. Moses, like the one that will deliver us out of misery. Or so the story goes... just to make Ma happy...

A woman steps into the room. She is tall, slender, and wears a yellow dress. It seems to be from the 1960s, undoubtedly old-fashioned. Her hazel eyes and pale skin glisten. Her curly brown hair is beautiful, but her feet do not touch the floor. Black wings protrude from her back and spread across the room. She floats next to Grams and whispers in her ear. Grams then strokes the woman's hand and smiles at me. The woman is strangely familiar, but I have never seen her before. Ma does not notice her presence. Are these the side effects of the meds? She anchors her eyes on me, and goosebumps seize me.

"I spoke with my sister, dear. She told me to tell you that to break the curse, you must sacrifice something." Gram says.

"Mother, with all due respect, please shut your mouth! My aunt has been dead for ages!"

Gram's sister! But why can't Ma see her? Perhaps superstition is real! If she is here to clarify this crap, then it is best to embrace Grams and her sister. They know better about all this… curse stuff. Gram's sister whispers in her ear for a long moment.

"Have you ever encountered people that stare at you? Like with an evil eye, *mal de ojo* as we say in Nicaragua?" Grams says.

Moses wakes up and cries. Mother gesticulates rocking movements. I copy her, and my child falls back to sleep within minutes.

"I don't think so, Grams, sorry. But sacrifice what?"

Her sister murmurs in her ear again. She doesn't ask me anything, nor will I reply to a specter. Of course, this can't be real, but even the unexplainable has a hidden meaning, even if I refuse to admit it. I do not believe in curses, but if this woman is here to help me, why should reality blind reason?

"She needs more information to know what you need to sacrifice. What about the time you went with your father to that ranch?"

"Mother! Stop! Enough with all these superstitions. Your sister is dead!"

"Ma, please be silent. Let her speak."

Ma moves to the window. Think… Think… Nothing comes to mind…

"Have you ever encountered a witch?" Grams asks.

"I don't remember…."

A nurse walks in to check Moses. Everything seems to be okay. She then examines me: no nausea, no vomiting, headaches are gone, and I can move my body now. Unfortunately, I can also feel things I'd wish not to feel… Flashbacks from the past, voices whisper in my ears, but I can't help but feel them. The nurse states visiting hours are over and that I must rest before discharge. Ma grabs her purse and rushes to the door. Grams touches me with her cold hand…

"Think hard, my dear. My sister wants to help you."

I shut my eyes and take a deep breath……

Flashes of the ranch, the mare, and a woman   *What is* *all this? all blurry*   *a face is blurry*   *a sinister laughter* *I scream for help, a light flash on my face, who is that!?*

THE BAD BLESSINGS

*Dancing   around the fire   a circle, dancing
creepy laughter   I can't see!......*

"Grams, do you know how these santeras look like?"

"They wear white gowns with a white turban, *elekes*...they are
necklaces that make rhythms, they dance *bembes*, the initiation
ceremony to heal and prophesize. They are from the *Lukumi*
religion, Catholicism, and of ancient African traditions. They
can heal, but they can curse."

*......A shadow dances, what does it say?   I   can't
understand it,   it moves something in my face
          but it is blurry, a little black face   Pa   moans,
Pa is that you again?   A horse... wait   I have seen her... an old
woman with a white gown, a necklace with beads of eyes, and... and she
dances and chants, incense swirls around her, that's what she was... that's
her, a santera, but how can this be!   Alice is that you?   Where is
my Moses? Is he is okay,   that evil laughter,   that old creepy
woman... santera stop please stop don't eat my Moses   she chops
and boils him... no don't eat him!   THE CURSE... THE
CURSE   her voice resonates   no......*

Grams waves her hand before my eyes. The visions?
... I wipe my watery eyes. Ma faces the door, detached. Grams
widens her eyes.

The darkness...where is the darkness? The woman?
Those flashes in my head, but now I can't even remember.
Perhaps I am tripping out.

"I am sorry, Grams, I don't think I remember someone like that...."

She squints and scratches her head. Her sister gives her a hug. She then smirks at me and flies towards the wall. Could all this be an illusion? Perhaps it is too much superstition for one day. A good rest will calm my nerves. My son is my only concern now, and my family, of course. But the visions continue to flash and flash, those eerie wails give me a headache.

"Believe my dear. Do it for your child." Grams says in a somber tone.

"Grams, I can't think right now."

"Remember this: Witches don't take requests, dear. They demand something in return." Grams says.

She grabs her purse and whispers in my ear.

"Usually, people go to them for healing. But they also curse those that hurt them...my sister did that. Tell me everything that happened on that trip. My sister senses something evil in your past, but only you can tell it." Grams kisses my forehead.

Ma gives me a kiss on the cheek, and she holds my hand with tears in her eyes. She rushes out of the room with Grams without saying a word.

In this pensive silence, my heartbeat reverberates in my ears, and the white walls shatter into a jigsaw puzzle. Some pieces show Pa, some show Grams, and some are our trip to the Estrada ranch. Faces, eyes, smiles, and scowls are all over the floor. Alice's eyes, the twins' smile, and the santera's demonic stare. The wind smashes the windows, and a shrieking howl blows into the room. The puzzle pieces clatter as they attach. The pieces stick faster and faster, and they seem to form an image of my face. Finally, the wind turns icy cold, the room darkens, and the moon illuminates the complete puzzle on the wall.

The puzzle depicts the Estrada ranch, the dead twins, the shadow man, the creepy cart, Alice, and that woman in white, all standing behind me. A blurry silhouette holds Moses. Who the hell can it be? My family stands next to me, but they are granite statues. What does all this mean? Nothing, I need rest. I want to be a normal mother. But something unexplainable battles inside me… I can't help it. Perhaps I am cursed. There is no other explanation. I am lost, that is the plain truth. I am not sure how all this is my fault, but somehow, I am liable. Grams is right. The answer is within me.

The road to Willicha has sand dunes with a few scattered bushes, just past Death Valley National Park. The misty green mountains are at the end of the long narrow road, and roadkill on the sides. I roll down the window, and an infernal blast of air broils my face. The steering wheel vibrates in my hands, but I am in control this time. Moses wakes up. He is likely hungry. No child deserves to endure this weary drive, but this is for my family and him. I rock him to sleep. Hopefully, this santera is alive; we can't die in this heat for nothing. His vitals are okay, but his skin is balmy. Oh, crap, what the hell! The A/C blows warm air. There is no signal in this wilderness. I stand in the middle of the trail to wave my phone, but still no signal. The horizon is blurry, and the wind is warm as a brick oven. If we continue without an A/C, he might suffocate. Amourville is about a day away.

Something lurks in the corner of my eye. The shadow man emerges from the sand; when will it stop bugging me? Its hands turn into tentacles. This is the worst time to not feel my legs, but I rush back to the car. The hot dirt burns through my shoe. Each step gets harder and harder. The specter is a few steps behind my neck… almost there, just a bit more… my throat tightens, and my legs are jelly. My finger reaches the door. The shadow swings its tentacle and rips a piece of my shirt. Finally, I hop in the car… First gear, and with a step on the gas, the car blows a trail of dust. Moses is okay.

In the retro visor, the shadow man stands in the center of the road, it then disappears in the cloud of dust. My heart beats fast and my body drowns in sweat. My back bleeds, but I am okay; we can't stop here. The signal returns and Google Maps ETA is an hour. Hang in there my dear, Olive Grove is much cooler. This will soon be over, I promise.

Willicha, situated somewhere between Chowchilla and Fairmead, is a third-world country, isolated from commercialism but unified by old traditions. Amourville is more progressive and wealthier than this place. Many of California's urban legends take place here, so it is no surprise why a witch would live around here. The old men with cigars give me an unpleasant stare; with only 1000 inhabitants, new faces are a threat to them. The roads are narrow and dusty, and the long tree branches grow all over the dilapidated buildings. If it weren't for the little city hall, the adobe church, and people on mules, this would be no better than a ghost town.

I pull to the curb to check on Moses. He is still a little warm but still alive. A black man wearing white clothes walks by. My phone is at 5% battery, the charger is broken, and it is almost sunset.

"Excuse me, sir, where can I find the Thomas Estrada estate?

He points to himself, and I nod.

"Me tinken… he die lo time… lo time, ah kill him, lon time." He gestures a shot in the head.

"Nobody lives there anymore?"

"Oh ya! A goo senora… a bii moter, bii mor dan all here! Teresa Estrada, bii moter." He takes a puff of his cigar.

"Where can I find Teresa Estrada?"

He gives me a bright smile filled with smoke and points to the end of the road.

"Go disa stret, Fires-sto-ne- all, all to ah, uh, con fils."

What the hell is con fils? His gestures seem to peel something. I pull up my phone and show him corn—that's what the town is known for, and it sounds like con. The black man nods erratically.

"Thank you so much!" I say.

He takes another puff of his cigar and waves.

The next street is Firestone. He said to go straight until I hit the corn fields, and then what? The ferry is much faster, but I can't even afford that right now. Well, back on the two-lane highway. The road is long and desolate, but Moses is alive; that's all that matters. Hopefully, they at least have water at this estate. The ranch should be cooler, but California's drought has dried our crops and lives.

The corn fields reflect the power of the sun. The rays melt our skin, and with no A/C, the warm wind is all we have left to breathe. The road gets blurry; I am so dehydrated. The car sways to the side… Shit! Can't keep my eyes open. Does this place even exist? We are going to die here…

There is something in the distance, a big sign, black with golden letters, but the words are too far to see. I step on the gas. The corn fields turn into vivid lily gardens, and the sweet smell elevates my posture. The sign reads, *Estrada Estate, Est. 1886*… finally we made it!

The creepy house is in the middle of a paradise of lilies and pastures. The foggy windows have blinds with smeared fingertips and the paint peels off the headers. Two massive Georgian-style columns–the only things that seem stable–hold a dilapidated pediment with grimy angels on each side. The hip roof and the creepy dormers give the sense that the house stares at me. The ranch is dead-silent, except for the eerie wind howl across the soulless field. If a ghost needs to take my life, so be it; this curse must end today. I take Moses out of the car for some air. He sneezes but seems okay. We are here… now what?

A young girl, no older than 12, gallops towards me on a majestic white horse. She is slim and pale with some shades of purple under her eyes, her blonde hair is nappy, her checkered shirt is clean yet old and faded, and her jeans have stitched holes. It seems as if she has never seen outsiders.

"Can I help you?"

"My name is Rose Rendar. We need water. My child might be sick."

She gallops back to the stables and then runs into the house. Moments later, she brings out two glasses of water. It does not matter where this water comes from. It moistens my dry mouth and cools our balmy skin. Now there is enough saliva in my mouth to speak…

"I am looking for Teresa Estrada. Does she live here?"

The young girl widens her eyes, "How do you know her?"

"I don't really know her, but she knows me. Is she alive?"

"Yes, she is my grandmother. I am Joysie. What is this for?"

This girl must be Alice's daughter, or could she be my half-sister?! She even looks a bit like Alice, despite her sickly appearance.

"Can you please tell her that doctor Rendar's daughter is looking for her?" She nods and rushes back to the house.

This isolation gives me goosebumps. We are cut off from the world. Who will care for my son after I die? Ah, this agony… seconds turn to minutes, and minutes turn to hours. Perhaps that girl is a ghost. In that case… Do I commit suicide to break this curse? Or what? Finally, the front door busts open. I press Moses to my chest.

"Rose…" a raspy sinister voice emerges from the dark interior, and my body shivers. An old woman with a twisted wooden cane steps out of the darkness. Her wrinkled sunburned skin, glistening yellow eyes, and ancient white hair, with everything else Grams told me……

The flashbacks…it is her, the santera!……

"I knew you would return someday." She coughs.

"You two know each other?" Joysie asks.

"I have known her for 12 years." Teresa says.

THE BAD BLESSINGS

I can't stare into her demonic eyes, I can't......

Father, Mother, Kashmir, Grams...   your voices, you all scream you guys burn where? hell?   No don't panic I am here to save you all   they beg me for help   stop please stop crying   their poor wails ring in my ears I need to go... no I am brave   family comes first   my son trusts me   I am tired of this life   I am the only one with power to change it......

"Then you must know what I am here for, Teresa."

Teresa nods and makes an evil chuckle. Joysie glances at both of us, baffled. As Teresa moves toward me, Joysie runs to the barn.

"I told you... bring me your blood, do you remember?" Teresa says.

"Yes..." My voice cracks.

Teresa bursts into laughter. Moses wakes, crying. She gives Moses a baleful smile with her golden teeth.

"This is your blood too?"

I nod and tighten my grip on Moses. Teresa waves her hands over him. She runs her long yellow nails over his body, then she places her nasty nails on my heart.

This is for you, my son, and the memory of the Rendars. Unfortunately, I cannot solve life's problems, but now you are all free...

9

Tell them not to kill me, tell them not to kill me!... Marcelo, can you hear me? Sherry traps me with no food, very little coffee, just one cigar a day, and nobody to talk to. She gives me medicine all day to put me to sleep. Big rocks shake in my head, and all they can give me are pills. That's all, pills… I want to see the lakes, the heavenly pastures, the volcanoes, that island in the lake, drink cacao, eat rice and beans, and smell the pure air of my Nicaragua. Marcelo, please save me. My wrists burn to open this rusty window, my only glimpse of freedom. This green room is tiny and stuffed with Sherry's yard sale odds and ends. The humid stench makes it hard to breathe, and specks of mold grow on the wall. My dilapidated cot breaks my back every night, and my joints hurt from stepping on this uneven floor full of bumps and cracks. I can't even walk here. My only comfort is to hear your voice and to write you letters…but you hardly reply.

Sherry wants to get rid of me. You must stop her because she is your daughter too! My 80 years of life can't end here, on a leash like a dog. Why should I please you? I want to please myself! This is the destiny of all rebellious women, loneliness. If you still have an inch of love, please rescue me Marcelo. I want to escape.

If you must go, I'll call you back later…bye. The old fool thinks he can escape me, but he will regret this neglect at a high price. A letter is the best form of communication. It shows how much effort the person puts into communicating thoughts and feelings. Sounds, words, and phrases echo in our minds and imprint in our hearts. If Marcelo does not answer my call, he won't ignore this letter. None of the pens in my drawer work. My quill is broken. This pencil has a little bit of graphite left. That means my emotions must stimulate him with the least amount of words. Marcelo hates to read.

There is an old photo of Marcelo at the edge of my desk. He is handsome and strong, and next to him is my beautiful little Sherry. My eyes glance at the scattered old photos. Cobwebs, dust, and longing cover them. Our wedding photo is still intact… Marcelo is so drunk, I must care for him, even if he beats me later… Sad memory, drunk on our wedding day. Oh, God! A wooden map of Nicaragua, my only souvenir, my only good memory.

It will be an honor to die in my land. Time to write, but nothing comes to mind… God, if you exist, please help me write the perfect letter.

Marcelo, please tell Sherry to let me go back… sounds like a good start. There must be a sharpener in this drawer, but something else catches my attention, an old metal thimble and thread. Brings back my dream of being a famous designer and make millions to travel the world, but also brings back the nightmare of marrying Marcelo, just to see my family eat.

Beautiful thimble, you preserve my hopes and aspirations, and even my mother's memory. Marcelo a good for nothing womanizer, Sherry needing food and you, thimble, providing for my family. I will forever be grateful for your loyalty… Marcelo is dead.

The crisp wind tightens my wrinkled face. The plants bend as it blows across the pastures and the tree branches rattle. The birds chirp like in my country, and a deep peace surrounds the veranda. This coffee is delicious, it relieves this uncontrollable shiver. Cardamom cakes are coffee's perfect companion, soggy with some crunchy hints. Peace, but this is fake peace… The white gate has that gigantic lock; supposedly, it is for my safety. Sherry wants to trap me, but she is crazy. The curse will destroy the Rendars. I can't let it destroy me.

Sherry wants to place me in a retirement home. Canasta is stupid, people bore me, and it's not Nicaragua. My end is near, and all my heart wants is coffee, cardamom cakes, cigars, and freedom. My only fear is to lay on my deathbed and discover that I never lived. That is why I must escape, to give my last days meaning, to experience the circle of life… or something like that, I don't know. Love is not as necessary as people think. It is better to be understood, heard, and remembered. But people prefer to suffer for love. I am done being here.

Some more coffee and a cigar sound good. This coffee is delicious, but not better than Nicaraguan mountain coffee. Father takes me to cut coffee beans on the foggy mountain slopes. The ambiance is cold, and the mist sticks to my skin like glue, but each breath is an enchanting dose of energy. The farmers are friendly and humble. A boy on the coffee plantation likes me, his name is Raimundo, I think, can't remember. Father commands me to stay away, but he is a nice boy. Father then presses his iron hand on my fragile arm. I can only look at the boy and say: "I'll be back to kiss you…one day, I will be rich." What a sad memory for a beautiful day. The feelings from the coffee plantation still disturb me after many years. It is hard to live, hard to escape, and everything I want is denied. Father takes me away from innocence, and Sherry takes me away from my last desire… To die in my homeland, happy.

Something taps me on the shoulder. Who can it be? Maybe, I am going crazy. Something taps me again… who is it?

"Excuse me, mam, you spilled all your coffee!"

A tall, handsome young man, maybe mid-30s, walks into the veranda from the other side of the fence. His blonde hair, sunburned skin, and eyes of heaven glisten like a god.

"Who are you?!" I say.

"I am sorry to jump in. My name is Jesus." He takes a towel from his pocket and kneels to clean the spilled coffee.

How could I drop my coffee? But did I drink it? Yes… um no… it's all over the veranda, Sherry will kill me with more and more sleeping pills! But I was drinking right? Oh, that memory on the plantation. So that's why it smells like pure coffee, silly me. But I am ok, I am fine… right?

"Thank you, young man."

"My pleasure. You seemed to be in deep thoughts."

"Deep thoughts? No, I was just thinking about what to make for dinner."

"I work the land next to your house…."

"Oh, I don't pay much attention then." I say with a stony expression.

"I pay attention to detail. I want to be a painter, to help those who can't hear or can't move to experience nature."

He has a strange dream for a farmer. But he speaks to me like a human being, much like Raimundo. He does not yell at me like Sherry or like my granddaughters. His gentleness is contagious. It becomes harder and harder to ward him off. It will break my heart to destroy his dream to be a painter. I can't be like father.

"You like to paint nature?" I ask.

"Yes. I capture beauty, even humans. Humans are beautiful."

"How? We are greedy."

"Humans are good. It is fear that makes them evil. But life is beautiful."

Young fool, his comedy calms my sorrow. But his optimism is impressive, his tone is full of passion, he is interesting...

"My dear boy, when you get to my age, you will realize that no matter what you do, people don't care about you. Humanity is evil by nature."

"I care about you."

¡La Sangre de Cristo!... Those words are lovely yet foreign, my only response is a smile. There are no words for his words.

"You would make a powerful painting." He says.

"Sweet young man. You will make a girl happy one day. Would you like some coffee?"

"Sure..."

He is full of vitality, never met anyone with such a positive view on humanity and art. As we sip our coffee, Jesus has a vigorous smile that lifts my soul, a smile that can only be seen once in life, the smile of... Freedom. My body wants to jump, run, hug the heavens, and scream: I am free! I am young again! I feel young. Coffee, good company, and nature... the recipe for happiness.

Why must he leave? He cares about humans. He paints. Why would he leave me without a word of hope? I wish he'd tell me he will be back, even if it is a lie.

"Tell me, why do you love to paint Jesus?"

"You don't seem to care…."

"Please tell me…." I insist. He sits on the stairs.

"Things are not the way they seem. There is always a hidden meaning, something deeper. Painting exposes the nectar of life and takes us into a different world."

Sherry might show up any moment, and she won't be happy about this encounter. He should leave, but all his expressions make me think and think. Beauty… the true meaning of life… love… painting… imagination. Jesus inspires me to live, and perhaps to…. I don't know, but he makes me feel good.

"Painting makes you escape?" I ask.

He squints and smiles at me. He is hard to fool, or so it seems.

"Yes! Without art, we would not escape pain."

"Where can I escape to?"

Jesus looks to the pastures, shuts his eyes, and takes a deep breath.

"Anywhere you can imagine!" He says.

"Nicaragua!" I yell.

He gets startled, but that smirk on his face confirms my feelings... Escape through art.

If Jesus has the desire to paint me, he can make me desirable to the eyes of others. They will feel my desolation, and they will buy the painting. Then they will look for me and finally take me out of this house... soon I'll be in my homeland. This meeting is not an illusion. Each sip of coffee warms my heart. I feel it... He is my escape, my only hope.

"Can you paint me?" I ask.

He thinks for a moment.

"Perhaps... after I finish my masterpiece."

"What is your masterpiece?"

"It is a big painting. It's a land where there are rainbows, animals speak, humans fly, and freedom is everywhere. No pain, no suffering, abundance of food, no sickness, God smiles in the sky, and the devil plays in the trees. This place has power over the mind... I think, I hope."

My hairs rise at the vivid description. It reminds me so much of Nicaragua.

"Where is this place?"

He looks around, nervous.

"Do you really want to know?" He whispers.

I nod, and he takes another glance.

"But you can't tell anybody. Not even your husband."

"My husband is dead. Please tell me." I whisper.

He strokes his hair back and moves closer to my ear.

"Some people think this place is a myth, but I have been there."

"I want to go. I want to be free." My voice cracks.

Jesus gives me a faint smile and pulls a piece of paper and a broken graphite from his jacket. He then sketches something.

Jesus shows me his drawing. It is a paradise, with some flowers, mountains, trees, and a lake in the middle, but with no sun and sky, just a layer above it… I don't understand. Is this his masterpiece? It is well sketched, but is it hell or heaven? Oh, I can't even think anymore.

"This paradise is beneath us. It is not of this world. It exists only to those that believe."

This young man has an amazing conviction. His words sound like a joke, but I just can't help but believe him.

"I don't believe you." I say.

He frowns and drops the sketch to the ground.

"Then it makes no sense to tell you about beauty and freedom. Maybe you are right, humans don't care."

I grab him by the arm before he gets up. How can I be so stupid?

"Are you sure about this place?" I ask.

"Your mind is powerful. If you can imagine it, you can believe it. Not everything we see is true. Not everything we don't see is fake."

What a wise young man. He must be a God or an Adonis. How sad, he understands the world, but perhaps nobody understands him. I want to understand him. Why do we imagine other worlds if this world is the only one that exists? Why is there heaven and hell? There must be a paradise, and he knows where it is. I will escape and be happy!

"Take me, please, I believe, I believe… I am sorry, it just sounds too good to be true, please believe me!"

"Do you have a shovel?"

I nod. Sherry must have one around the garden.

"You must dig a hole; your beautiful garden would be a perfect location. But you can only enter the hole at night, and I'll show you the way." He whispers.

"Why my garden?"

"This place only appears around nature...."

"I'll get started now and go in tonight. But where will I find you?"

"I'll be in your garden, don't worry, trust me." He kisses my hand like a gentleman. "Not a word to anyone. Make sure nobody sees."

He puts on his hat and jumps the fence. Jesus waves, then he disappears through the trees.

Good lord! It's 6pm and Sherry closes the store at 8pm! That hole must be ready before Sherry sees it. Jesus's sketch floats in my head. I can feel it...but Rose and Sherry need me. Will they cry to know I am gone? Or will they cry with joy? Poor Rose, that curse consumes her and makes her see things, yet she disbelieves. Her child will suffer, and I don't want to stay around to see her fate. I will go dig...

But no, Sherry! How can I disappear? That is cruel, a mother should never leave a child behind. But she traps me in this house like a bird. My wings bleed, and soon even freedom will feel like pain. I am not a mother anymore. I am a bird. She can suffer, lousy daughter. The need to solve the problem of life is above family and love. Freedom is the solution to life.

This is Ruben's old shovel. It is bent, but this will do. It's hard to believe that our garden—Sherry truly keeps it beautiful—has a paradise beneath it. Like an iceberg, beauty is at the bottom, ugliness is always on top.

Dig, dig, and dig… a spasm crushes my back, but I want freedom.

Dig…dig…dig…dig…dig…dig… The shovel is heavy, there is barely any dirt out. But no giving up! The smell of wet dirt makes me sneeze. My body aches, but freedom is near; I can smell it. Dig…dig…dig…dig…dig…dig…

There is my hole! My hole! Not too big, not too small, but it seems appropriate. Only a few things in my life bring me happiness: Raimundo, Marcelo's death, Nicaragua, coffee… and this hole. First, I wonder… then I fear… then I doubt, and I am not crazy, but we all go crazy when we dream and dream… now my dream comes true.

"Hello paradise, can you hear me?" I yell into the hole.

No response. Perhaps the hole needs to be bigger. "Hello… Hello…" Still no response. This is strange, maybe Jesus knows the way. It's 7:50pm; Sherry and Rose must not find out. If they discover this, Jesus will be mad, and my freedom will be buried forever.

The bushes make a disturbing rattle. A shadow appears and my heartbeat rises. When the shadow moves into the last bit of sunlight, Jesus appears. He hugs me and then turns his attention to the splendid hole. Jesus looks at me with a serious expression.

"Do you really believe in this paradise?"

"I believe in this paradise with all my heart and mind."

His expression does not change. Honestly, a little doubt lurks within me about the existence of this paradise, but it makes no sense to turn back now. Perhaps paradise does not exist, but I must pretend… What if it does exist? I want to know…

"Does anybody know about this place?" He asks.

"No…"

Sherry yells out my name from the kitchen. Jesus restlessly searches for an exit.

"I'll be back, don't let anybody see it!" He says.

Jesus jumps the fence and disappears into the darkness. It's too hard to cover this hole again. What do I do? What do I do?... Think…

Coffee! Sherry loves coffee after a hard day's work. She usually falls asleep after her night coffee. I prepare the coffee as she likes it, decaffeinated with half and half, with just a bit of sugar. Sherry walks into the garden.

"What is this? Mother! Did you do this?" She yells.

THE BAD BLESSINGS

Sherry examines the hole for a moment, and after a few curses and damnations—the pastor will ask for more money for all those prayers—she shoves the dirt back into the hole.

No! How can she? That evil cunt! Bad daughter! Jesus will think I betrayed him, and my eyes won't see paradise.......

Oh, why are these decisions so hard!   Why?   She is my daughter, but I hate her!   I hate her!   She is just like Marcelo, selfish and ungrateful   my hole,   my freedom Please God help me! Kill her, that's it yes,   if she wants to ruin my life and kill me slowly then I must do it faster than her

I will not settle   I cannot be a victim

all my life people stepped all over me,   oh my little Rose now I see why you are a bitch   you just don't bend,   you fight   you keep your chin up   and that's why you will break that curse   I hope she is ok,   oh God what a waste of coffee maybe I should put a bit more   Sherry you ungrateful woman, after all I did for you,   you bury my hopes and dreams!   Should I? No I will regret it then   Should I not?

No, I will regret it too!   I don't know, life is too much of a problem, I can't solve it!   But it is now or never!   My decision is clear......

My reflection shines on this clean butcher knife. That's me, the only one with the power. Sherry fills the hole… I move closer and closer. The cold grass tickles my frozen feet, but my steps are subtle and slow. If she turns around, I am dead… Almost near her, just a few more steps. Here I go; this is for my freedom. Only a few more steps… I hold up the knife, but where should I stab her? Stomach? Chest? Face? Perhaps her mouth? I don't know. My arms tense and my legs are noodles. This is not right. I am not a murderer.

The ghastly voices of father, Raimundo, and Marcelo echo in my head. A few feet away from her…. Nobody will ruin my last happy days, not even Sherry. My hole is almost covered! No! No! No!

Sherry turns around, I swing the knife across her stomach and her guts drop on the grass. She gives a loud shriek, and finally collapses.

"I am covered in the blood of Jesus Christ… I am covered in the blood of Jesus Christ… I am covered in the blood of Jesus Christ." I say to myself.

I am very ill, so ill my mind can't think, my eyes itch. I don't know, but lord… Is this the price of freedom... death? What is done cannot be undone. My hands, mind, and heart make a choice for the first time in my life. Then I am not sick, my mind can make decisions without anyone in my way.

Not one tear sheds from my eyes; soon, I will be in paradise. Sherry needs a proper burial. I must dig another hole before Rose gets here. Jesus should also be here any minute. My bony hands can't even drag her. The more I gasp, the less my body responds. There is no other choice, I push the cadaver into my hole.

I drop on my knees, the severed corpse stares at me. "Sherry… Sherry… Sherry…" Each time in a higher tone, but it does not respond. Sherry is dead. Hastily but with the utmost care, my shivering hands cover her with dirt until the cadaver disappears… forever.

This great deed is done. Blood swirls down the drain until there is no evidence at all. I better go dig another hole before Jesus gets here. The bushes wiggle again, it must be Jesus! I rush over to the garden and begin to dig another hole. God's speed and strength runs through me. Minutes later, there is a new hole in the ground, not as big as the first one, but it's a hole.

Jesus jumps the fence. He scouts the garden and comes across the pile of dirt from the first hole. He examines it for a moment. Lord, please grant me passage to this paradise.

"Why are you digging another hole?"

I pretend not to hear him. He reaches for my hands and gently strokes them.

"Why are you digging another hole?" In a stern tone.

"Sherry…my daughter, she… she covered the first one while I was making coffee. But I will be done soon, I swear!" I stutter.

Jesus releases my hands and crosses his arms. I continue this painstaking dig.

"Stop, please stop." He says.

I drop the shovel and wipe the sweat from my eyes. The gazebo lights automatically switch on and cast a silhouette over him. His menacing stance makes a whirlpool in my stomach. Jesus is too intelligent to be fooled. Sometimes, age is not wisdom.

"Dishonesty is not allowed in paradise...." He says. I lower my face.

"If you lie, that means you don't believe. If you don't believe, you can't go into paradise!" His voice cracks.

An anvil drops on my chest. My pleas are not enough, my thousand apologies are unacceptable. Jesus goes down on his knees and whimpers into his hands. Even in her last breath, Sherry destroys my goals! My God, my God... Is all this even happening? Jesus gets up and slouches towards the gate. My heart breaks to see him leave.

"Wait! I still believe in beauty and art!" I yell.

"I am beauty and art. I was your savior. I was everything you wanted, but you lied. In time you will hate what you always had... Greed."

Jesus jumps over the fence and disappears into the darkness. In this garden I die, the bushes kill me, all because I was digging for a garden without any bushes. I go, Judas Iscariot, to cut bushes, to find death, ah that's right, you are my father...

Cardamom cakes dipped in coffee are the best comfort. Rose is not here, perhaps I should ask her to come. What if Jesus returns to kill me? The living room phone is out. The phone in Sherry's room works, but something instantly captures my gaze. Plane tickets on Sherry's dresser. She and I are the passengers, and the destination: Nicaragua! *¡La sangre de Cristo!* My deepest desire is in my hand, but I can't touch it. Why can't I?... Greed. Paradise? That is in our eyes. Hell, it's here in front of us...

The river sparkles, and its thunderous current rings in my ears. I can barely hear you. This is not heaven. This white garment means nothing to me. Nature is the best place to reflect on life. I still think of freedom. What is freedom? To me, it's Nicaragua, or at least to choose where and when I want to die. We can't always get what we want because we have some control; others create circumstances, and then those circumstances affect us. We can't escape those unwanted circumstances unless we live in a lonely island. Freedom is, therefore, an illusion. There will always be something that stops us. Men, women, children, work, politics, weather, illness, the mind... and death control us.

Curses... they do exist. We have one. I don't think it will be broken. It requires too much faith, hope, and love. Those are three things the Rendars do not have, just a little bit, not enough. I know how to break Rose's curse. But I will not say anything because they will put me in the ward to play canasta with old people. The Rendars need to learn a lesson; don't think of your own hell and blame others for it. Will they learn? No. Although Rose stands by what she believes—even if she is wrong many times—she never owns up to her faults. Instead, she thinks she is perfect and blames others for her issues. I hope she learns her lesson.

Are you not going to say anything, Marcelo? So that's it, you stay quiet, no opinion! Marcelo, I hate you, you ruin everything. Leave, stop controlling me! Stop! Do not force me to jump off this bridge. It would be better than going back to that spongy white room, but… it's too early for death. Perhaps there is a chance to escape to Nicaragua. Oh yes, believe me, hope flows in me like the river. Hope can't be lost; it keeps us young. Do you know why Marcelo? … because it does not come from reason; it's just imagination. Fine, don't believe me, keep that resting bitch face. I am going to jump. Here they come, those people in white. Bye Marcelo, I never thought you would betray me. Happiness is when you don't love things… things cannot love you back, they don't even know you exist. Love yourself, you know you exist…

10

The icy ambiance stiffens my frail body. The dense humidity sticks to my skin like glue, and the stench of mold clogs my nose like a bad cold. The living room is antique and eerie. Joysie must be miserable to live in a lifeless place. A still silence vibrates through the house. The only sound comes from the nerving drops from a faucet. Teresa points to a dark corridor, and the vivid memories return. She enters the hallway with a dim candle, but the darkness swallows her. It pains me to put Moses through this wicked situation, but it is my duty as a good mother. Perhaps it is time to have faith now that my spine tingles and everything is dark. My hand trembles as it brushes through the freezing wall. It is the only way to know I am alive. Teresa's sinister chuckle echoes in the corridor, my body cringes. A dot of light appears at the end. Is this what people call hope? Or is this a hopeless end? The white dot becomes larger, and my eyes squint from the blinding luminance. We reach the end of the corridor, and the dot is an old flickering bulb next to a coffin-like door. Teresa stands by the door, ominous and pale… The 12-year-old memories return… all because of stubbornness… Now it is time to die for my mistakes.

"Give me a moment, please." I implore.

"Don't worry, he will live free." Teresa says.

"What will you do to him?"

She rolls her eyes.

*...... my son,   forgive me for bringing you into this world
        but I rather kill myself than give you a curse   this is the
least I can do   for giving you, life   a life without any
meaning a life where you will be happy   and also sad
        I must rip you from my heart   but of course, complete sadness
and complete happiness is never possible, my happiness is that you won't
be cursedFather, why?   All for a woman?   You killed your
daughter   and desolated your grandchild...   mother if your God
exists, please   ask him to forgive me   Moses......*

"What are you waiting for?" Teresa asks.

"I can't leave my child...."

"Now that you entered the house, you must complete the ritual
within two days." She widens her yellow eyes, "And if you leave
the estate before the ritual, the curse stays forever."

"But my child!"

"I don't care about him...."

"Hard to believe you care about anything."

"Oh, I care, I care...and that's why I cursed you."

"What the hell did you put on me?"

"Something more powerful than the love of a family. You have been warned...."

She heads back into the corridor. We are now alone, the light flickers, and spine-chilling footsteps echo in the cold darkness. I rush into the corridor with only a bit more faith, but I am unsure what to have faith in.

The magic hour is a gorgeous purple sky with hints of orange over the perfect horizon, a flawless line, unaltered by the eagles that flap their wings through the cirrus blue clouds. The sun sets over the land, and the rays stretch across the green pastures, like a lyrical dream. A dream, of course, surrounded by a nightmare. The nightmare of paying for someone else's mistakes. This must be the worst death, disgraceful and unjust. My pride is down, death is but a yearning, and Moses? What will happen to Moses? We are in the middle of a holy hell with no escape and only two days left. This is the worst nightmare.

Joysie brushes a white horse in the paddock. Then a black horse strolls over to her white horse, and they caress each other. Animals have unconditional love. Unlike humans, they don't have ulterior motives.

I know that white horse. Those ocean eyes drown my gaze. I move towards the paddock and a cascade of memories drops on me. It's you! It is you, little mare!... You are so big, I remember your painful birth, but you are alive and happy. I envy you, surrounded by pain, yet happy with someone who loves you.

"Who gave you this horse?"

"It was a gift from my father. My mother left it behind."

"Where is your mother?"

"She left for Port Granada when I was little. I don't remember much. I never knew her name...."

"I am sorry to hear that."

"It was her fault, I think... she was with another man."

"It is probably best you did not know her."

"If I would to see the man she left my Pa for, I would kill him with my own hands."

She gestures a jab. What a precocious little brat. If only she knew the truth...I don't blame her. I would feel the same.

"So would I...." I whisper.

"My grandma and I suffer every day. I quit school to work with her here, but I don't know what to do if she dies." Her voice cracks, "We barely sell any crops, and everything my Pa had, my mother took it with her."

She strokes the white horse with a sullen expression. Poor girl, her most vulnerable years are nothing but a pile of rotten crops. She is like an animal, trapped in a cage. Her grandmother must control all her thoughts to keep her here.

One day she will realize that nothing is permanent, that hate, and love are useless, and she will rebel and become evil. But hopefully, she will become as strong as me. If she becomes like Teresa, she should die… she should stay ignorant and malnourished for her own good.

It's hard to not admire these horses. Their majestic affection appeases my senses and clears my mind. Perhaps these horses reflect the one thing missing in my life, unconditional love.

"Can I?" I ask. Joysie nods.

Its white skin is silky velvet, and each stroke soothes the palm of my rough hand. Its long mane is a soft paintbrush, thin and flowy, and her eyes are as deep and mysterious as my past. The mare's energy vibrates all over my skin.

The white mare then gallops to her mate. The horses lick each other and lift their tails sideways.

"They are so cute, aren't they?" Joysie says.

"Yes, there is more love between animals than humans."

"That's true…."

"Will they have foals?" I ask.

"They are both females…but maybe, nature is mysterious…."

My jaw drops, and words parch in my throat. Animals see no difference, no hate, no jealousy, no restrictions, and no traditions, just the act of love. I want to be an animal and detach from this nasty society. Society distorts everything and makes it hard to be, to live, and to love. In nature, love is love just like… Laura! Yes, Laura… this can't be a coincidence. The admiration of these horses paints her image, her voice… My hairs raise.

Laura can care for Moses. But damn! No reception! How ironic, I never thought I'd say this, but I need Laura; she is my last hope. Hope……

Laura,   why did I do this to you?   You would be here with me, would you? I know you would,   Beloved…   I am sorry…   my stubbornness, my fear has led me here, the denial of my true persona   with time we hate what we always had   I always had your love and   fuck how could I   you were my unconditional love   forgive me ,   Laura probably forgot about me, with her body and charisma, anyone would fall for her,   but she chose me   but   but   how do I reach her?   It is a one day trip to the big city   maybe this little horse girl can reach her   I don't know, somehow horse girl doesn't need to know everything… she is smart yet naive

but she can help me   faith…   this is faith,   that Laura comes and cares for my son   could that happen?   No, not really   But   it   must   happen Maybe, if I try,   if I believe… that is faith…   this girl still has a good heart, this act will ensure her heart stays pure and innocent, for my son and for my family   I am not doing what is fair,   but what is right, what is best for us all……

"Oh shit, I… I feel sick, sick! My stomach! Can you help me?" I yell.

My body shivers, and I slowly go down on my knees with a tight grip on Moses. My grunts are as loud as my labor pains. Joysie covers her ears and moves around like a clumsy chicken.

"What's wrong with you? What do I do? What…"

"I need medicine… I ran out of insulin, and unless I get some, I will die."

Moses cries, I trudge to my car to ensure that she believes this illness, or at least to make her pity me. There is no signal and no gas, but there are horses and papers available. So, my only choice is to send Laura a letter; the most intimate way to pour my soul.

Joysie will buy this act. She sounds smart, but she is naïve. Joysie reaches my car, out of breath and disoriented. Please don't faint now little girl…

"I'll get my grandma to help you!"

"No! My father wants to buy this ranch, but your grandmother disagrees. You won't need to work, and you can go back to school, perhaps a better life for both of you… she needs time to think. Leave her alone.…"

"I don't understand. She never told me anything."

"Trust me. Just leave her alone, don't give her any trouble."

"How can I trust you? I don't know you…."

"I am dying Joysie…."

"Then what do you want me to do?"

"Can you deliver a letter to the big city?"

She nods with a sense of insecurity.

"In how much time?"

"Maybe… a day, Mary is pretty fast." She stutters.

"Please deliver a letter. My friend is the only one that can bring me medicine. My life and my baby's depend on it." I gasp for air.

Joysie squints and exchanges glances between the house and me. My wails and pleas seem to work on her. But will she die on the road? Will Laura arrive? Whatever the outcome, my heart is ready.

"Do you have the letter?" Joysie asks.

"I'll write it…."

"I can leave at dawn, so grandma, don't stop me. Mary, my white horse, is the fastest of them all."

"One day? I might not make it, but it's my only hope."

"Will you be, ok?"

"No, I will die unless my friend can bring me medicine… but I guess I'll be fine.…"

Joysie runs back to the barn. The worst good thing a girl can be is sweet and innocent. She doesn't pick up on the purpose of my visit, nor does she perceive my lie. But why do I trust an innocent girl? I am absolute. I am selfish. I am stubborn. I am like a man. But today, I am faithful. Today I am humbled and weak…but this is the right thing to do. In desperation, even the strongest are weak.

"Don't tell your grandmother. I don't want to worry her." I yell.

"She doesn't come out of the house. She is sick."

Each curve within the letters carries the shivers of agony, joy's restlessness, and anger in the bold words. She will feel my beating heart in her hands and hear my loud words……

"Dear Laura, I hope this letter finds you well. This is random, I know, and perhaps you moved on, but you are the only person alive to help me. Everyone in my family is gone, and I am dying. My son needs someone to take him out of here. I have no phone signal or gas in my car. We are stranded on a ranch about two hours away from Willicha. I can't explain too much, but his life is in danger, and here you will understand why I turned my back on you. Please, I beg you, help me. If I die, my son will be left alone in this desolation. If you rip this letter, I'll understand. I will die with the satisfaction that you loved me. Remember you promised that

you would never hate me, no matter what. Please rescue me if you want. I'll be here waiting, love……"
Regards, Rose Rendar.

The car roof light shuts off. Moses unsettles, and a cold wind blows across the ranch, is this a tempest? Joysie demands that we enter the house. That is the best idea because Moses can't be out in the cold. I place the letter in her callous little hands. She hides it in her jacket.

The house is warmer than outside, despite the cold humidity. Loose fibers stick out of the sofa cushions, and with every desire not to, I sit on the sofa with Moses. The camel sofa makes a loud squeak that breaks the eerie silence. Any movement can collapse the frame into dust.

The paint peels off the lofty beige walls like claw scratches. The walls have massive tapestries—one depicts the moon kissing the sun, and the other a human hand with candles and skeletons dancing around. The crystal chandeliers give off a dim illumination, with an occasional flicker. There is a table with a small black doll in a white garment with two candles, and my hairs rise at the bizarre setup, much like an altar. There is a table at the center of the living room with many old photos---Pa and Mr. Estrada shake hands, and there is Alice, bitter and repressed; I have no respect for her now. An old, faded painting of Eros and Psyche hangs at the end of the living room. It is dusty and tilted sideways. Laura and I… She likely has a better life without me, she has no troubles. Will I disrupt her happiness? The love of Eros and Psyche, perhaps a fantasy, nonetheless it is love, love is possible… Anything is possible…

Moses feeds on my breast. The light from Joysie's candelabra fades as she walks up the stairs. There isn't much hope except for Laura's return. Two knight statues guard an open door underneath the Eros and Psyche painting. The chandeliers go out. When the light returns, Teresa stands under the door frame like a corpse. Her yellow eyes glisten in the darkness. My body tenses and my eyes roll towards Moses, he is now asleep. My eyes look up again, but my jaw tightens; Teresa disappears from the door. She wants to scare me to death. It is time to test this faith or the existence of this God. Anything helps right now.

A shriek resonates as the knight moves its rusty leg. The other knight shakes its rusty limbs and thumps into the floor. The knights skulk towards me, is this witchcraft? The chandeliers flicker and flicker, and the knights speed their phantasmagoric movements. The surrounding candles give a hideous orange glare. This is a witch's circle. The knights are close, their rusty rattle tickles my ears and vibrates my teeth. Moses whimpers, and the knights aim their spears at us. My heart beats faster and faster. Sweat cascades over my body, Moses cries louder, and the urge to run rushes through my legs. The tip of his spear blurs in my eye; there is no escape……

I never thought of this moment,   but   help me,   take pity of me,   I don't know what else to say   save me,   now is the time I ask you,   now is the time I recognize you,

> *take me but save my child   how do they talk to you,*
> *how do you grant things   To you praise be given,   send a*
> *miracle, a lightning bolt strike down this evil and I promise to have faith*
> *I promise to   to   to   believe……*

The knights retract their weapons and plod back to their original position. The wind unlatches the windows, and the curtains flap like wings. A disturbing wolf's howl echoes across the room. All lights go off except for the yellow moon. Its gloom is so bright every crater is visible against a blue gradient night. The living room is now silent, except for the cricket chirps. The moon's shimmer reveals the black doll on the floor with all the scattered photos. This is not a dream or reality; I can't find an explanation. Perhaps this is the power of prayer, that's my only consolation. Now I understand Ma's fervor.

A rooster crows, and the rays that creep through the clouds tickle my eyes. Moses! He is in my arms, alive and well. The house is still ghost-silent… Footsteps thud, the ceiling cracks, the furniture stretches… The supernatural is wonderfully meaningless. Only faith can provide console, although faith can't answer what we don't understand. The barn door is open. May this God protect Joysie.

Laura will come, I think… why can't things be certain? But this uncertainty impels me to have…faith. We need to get some fresh air.

The red sun sets in the sky, as red as my desired blood. The wind sweeps across the pastures with a strong punch, all leaves bend to the wind's will, and an uneasy peace roams the estate. I want to cry, yet not a tear drops down. Perhaps, sorrow has come to a truce with my existence, but do I even exist? Existence is a hoax. This truce is a hoax. I am now alone with this empty shell, my body, that bends like the pastures and accepts reality. I give up. My mind is blank; what do I do next? Does my body still function? I don't know, it's meaningless anyway. Finally, Moses falls asleep, and Teresa walks onto the veranda.

"One more day Rose. Tomorrow by nightfall, you are cursed forever."

"Why did you curse me?"

"All your father came to do that day was to betray my son."

"What?"

"After Thomas discovered Alice's affair, he killed himself. Alice, that whore! She left with another man. I stayed with my Joysie, starving. Ruben killed my family, and now I will kill his."

"I have nothing to do with his dealings!"

"An eye for an eye, a family for a family. I can sense you are just like him. The Rendars are a disgrace. I don't know why my son kept him as a friend."

"Don't hurt my child. He has nothing to do with this."

"I am not responsible for him…."

Teresa walks back into the house. I lock myself in the hatchback of my car and wrap Moses in my jacket. We might freeze, but my car is safer than that living room. Moses is warm, but my body shivers. What a unique first experience of motherly love.

Teresa's heart is full of hate yet empty of blame. I would do the same if someone hurt my family. Her words, however, suggest despair and fear. There must be more to her eagerness to break this curse. I have become too hopeful, and it's meaningless. Pa's stigma breaks and bends me into a better shape… A shape that sees the best in people or a shape that rejects reality.

Light peeks behind the hills, golden rays stretch over the pastures, and the glorious sun shines above the land, the birds sing a lyrical chorus. My eyes squint at the glimmering heat. I rush over to look at the fields, but no signs of Joysie…….

Those times, a supernatural effort, to not break the glass, of all the things broken in my life, I failed,   when I look to the sun and hide my face, when the moon gives her glimmer, my pain is revealed, but of course,   sure   my end has come   that is why   there is joy and shame in my head and mind…they can't be the same anymore, they never were… I lost what I wished   but it is best to welcome death,   that is reality, the reality where I can be where I dreamt   who cares since it is all worthless   if I do there is regret   if I don't do regret too   bullshit, I give up everything……

A black shape appears on the horizon, and a trail of dust gathers over the field. I place my hand over my eyes… I can't believe it. Is this another illusion?

It's Joysie! I can't believe she made it! Her majestic mare thunders across the ranch with a loud neigh. Joysie stops at the paddock but doesn't acknowledge me. She then walks towards me with her face down. Even a lie is much better than prolonged uncertainty. My legs tremble.

"What did she say? Did you find her?" I gasp.

She wipes the sweat from her eyes.

"I gave her the letter…but she said she was not sure."

A cascade of cold water freezes my body. Fuck it… She has a new love or can't remember me…fuck it, if that is her decision, she must have a good reason for it. Loneliness is the fate of all those who have hope and those who love.

"I am sorry. She read it, but her face looked like she did not care. I don't know."

I dip my face into my hands.

"Let me get you to a hospital; you will die!" Joysie says.

"I am already dead. But thanks, I want to be alone."

Joysie frowns and runs back to the house. If Joysie's innocent face cannot bend Laura's heart, then nothing will. Moses needs his last breastfeeding.

The wind blows, and thunder rolls across the land. I sit on the veranda for a last breath of air. In a word, life is: Meaningless. It is useless to think and think, express, believe, and hate when others don't feel what you feel. If this is a story, well, I am tired of it. It should end right now. It is, however, not a story. It is my sad reality, only death can change it.

Joysie's words echo in my ears… Laura can still arrive, but she is just not sure. Hopeful until the end, why not? It does not hurt to hope anymore because loneliness is my fate. Teresa opens the door.

"Why did you get Joysie involved?"

"If she knew anything, she would have killed me already…."

"Give me your blood! End this now!" She cringes on her teeth.

"Wait, someone will be here for Moses… wait."

She sneers and steps back inside…….

Laura won't come, why do I keep saying this to myself,   no more hope, stop Rose, stop, she has a better life, you messed up yours, this is what you chose!   Maybe, just maybe, Laura keeps her promise no, she won't,   Laura has the right to be happy   I have the right to honor my family, yeah, that's it   I forgot, honor my family   this is for my son   but it is fine, I will die knowing that Laura is the love of my life, she just did not make it in time. She went after her happiness like she promised   Why does it even matter? I won't be here......

The grey clouds extinguish the sun and my hope. Teresa steps out with an eye necklace and a blue turban.

"The ritual is ready, hurry!" She says, anxious.

"Wait. Just wait, someone will come...."

"You don't even believe in your own hope, do you?"

"I do believe...."

Laura will not show. I just want to hold Moses for a little more. But hugs won't break the curse. Joysie steps onto the veranda, disturbed by Teresa's creepy garment. This innocent horse girl is my last source of comfort. I place Moses in her bony arms.

"Don't let hate consume your good heart." I whisper.

"Why are you giving me your baby?"

I stroke her head and give Moses a kiss.

The wind blows the remnants of my being. My feelings? They are shit. Forget the world, forget religion, tradition, Amourville, my family, and even Laura! The world is an illusion that casts shadows before our eyes. We are fooled daily; some realize the joke, and others die with illusions.

I am done. It's all my fault, and until the end, I realize this is life. I feel happy yet so sad, but damn why? If any good human speaks to me, my happiness and sadness will purge out, and I'd be dead either way…

Teresa opens the coffin-like door at the end of the corridor. My body hunches to keep my head from hitting the cold adobe ceiling. My breath resonates around the narrow walls. Walls in every dark direction with little room to breathe and no escape.

There is a shrine filled with candles. Three candles to the right, to the left, and three in the middle. Behind the candles, thin African dolls with feathers and white eyes stand in a circle, and the same black doll with a white robe and turban from the living room sits in the middle of the circle. Above the doll, the same photo from Pa's drawer stands with two blue candles. But this one has all of us completely visible. Above our photo lies a cement head with eyes, nose, and mouth made from shells. Teresa burns incense from a hand candelabra, it has that eye, that eye… it follows me, it glistens, eerie, and omniscient. What does it see? What does it want? You look and look, but you see nothing… Now you have me… but you will never look inside me, nothing destroys me unless I let it, not even an evil eye. Eyes, they hold the truth, but even the truth is seen by different eyes. The incense stifles my nose.

She takes out a dagger and waves it above the candles. Teresa makes a creepy rhythmic chant and raises her hands up and down. She then shakes her hips and chants louder and louder. Teresa pulls me to the center of the room. My body is jelly, and a cascade of sweat drops over me. She tosses seeds to form a circle and waves the dagger all over my body; the devil is possessing her. Teresa aims the dagger at my stomach…

"Rose! Rose!" Joysie yells from the living room.

Teresa stops the ritual. But with the strength left in me, I rush out of the room.

"Come back!" Teresa yells.

I rush out, disoriented and out of breath. Then, as my vision clears, my mouth drops, and my eyes widen.

Laura stands outside her car. I run to hug her. The hug is not as tight as the last time we saw each other but perfect enough for this moment. My hands caress her soft curly hair, but she maintains a morose expression.

"Why did you come?" I ask.

"Because I made a promise. I don't hate you, but I came to see if I still love you…." Laura says.

"This is all my father's doing. You and my family are just casualties…."

I lower my gaze, but Laura lifts my chin. Hopefully, she still has a soft side. Hopefully, this encounter doesn't kill

Laura's little speck of love. But whatever she sees in this place will question her beliefs if she has any.

"How do I know you still love me?" Laura says.

"I risked an innocent girl's life because I have faith in you."

"You are as stubborn and selfish as the last time I saw you!"

"I settled for sorrow, thinking I could handle it, thinking it was the right thing to do. But now, I realize I was wrong all along. Death is changing me…."

"You broke my heart, Rose."

"And life broke me. I don't ask you to forgive me. Please help my son, I beg you."

Laura walks over to the veranda and strokes Moses. Joysie takes a few steps back, but I nod at her with a faint smile. Teresa steps outside, out of breath and distraught. She gives Laura a contemptuous sneer.

"Who are you?" Teresa asks.

Laura turns towards me, "I can see why your life is in danger, Rose." Laura says.

"Rose, give me your blood to break the curse, hurry."

"What curse?" Laura asks.

Laura looks back at Teresa. Moses begins to cry.

"The curse I gave her for her father's stupidity." Teresa turns to Joysie. "Her father is the man your mother loved instead of your Pa…"

Joysie's eyes fill with tears. Poor little girl, the truth will muddle her.

"If we don't break this curse, your son and my Joysie will be cursed too." Teresa's voice cracks.

Joysie and Moses whimper.

"Get this kid away from me!" Joysie says.

Joysie hands Moses to Laura. Joysie then storms into the house. Teresa's glossy eyes confirm that even the darkest monsters have a heart. She genuinely cares for her granddaughter, not just for revenge.

Laura walks towards me. She carries Moses with a keen gentleness. If a monster has a heart, then much more an angel… There I go, hopeful when I shouldn't…

"Your family was cursed? By your father?" Laura asks. I nod.

"You never told me Rose!"

"I never believed in curses or anything, not even in love, until I met you. I was afraid you would think I was crazy, and I hid behind my family, thinking they would solve my internal struggle…I thought I was absolute. But now, after chasing the answers to life's problems, I find nothing… I find deception… I find death…."

"You should have told me. We choose who we love, but we don't decide how they are. Acceptance is true love. You should have had faith in love."

"Forgive me Laura. After I die, can you tell him my name?"

"Why must you die?"

"Because I carry the curse. 12 years ago, the witch asked for my blood. I need to sacrifice myself for my family and Moses… I must pay for my Pa's decisions…."

Laura begins to whimper, "I forgive you. I will care for this blessing."

It is not forgiveness I care for, but for my child. How could I leave them alone in this cold world? How could I be so selfish? This is not a happy ending, yet here we are, crying together. This love is the best there is. I would never choose another.

"I will raise him to love who you were…my love, a brave girl…." She says.

We walk back to the dark house, holding our cold soft hands. I love her. She is not mine; I am not hers. We are a temporary exchange of energy that will last forever. I can't cry. I shouldn't cry. She cries with tears, and I… with hopeful thoughts, with my truest deep love.

The day is almost over, and not even love can stop the inevitable… death.

"When he grows up, tell him…." Laura interrupts me.

"Don't worry, my love…."

Such a beautiful sight before my death. Teresa pulls me by the arm, and Laura's image disappears in the house's darkness. Joysie wipes her tears and stands in our way.

"Why will her curse kill me too?" Joysie asks.

Teresa strokes her hair, but Joysie pushes her away.

"Why?" Joysie demands.

"Because curses don't end, they pass on. All I want is the best for you. Trust me, dear."

Joysie evades Teresa's hug. I have nothing but pity for this little girl. Perhaps Teresa is right; greed and revenge are families' worst curses. Joysie lowers her head and steps out of our way.

Teresa resumes the ritual. She pulls my hands towards the altar. The candles blur, and Teresa places the dagger in my right palm. The blade's pressure burns my skin, and blood spills out of my hand. The light in the candelabra extinguishes, and blood oozes out of the eye. Life was good……

I have faith, I have faith   life was a good experience
*   short with problems, but I guess good   I have faith that*
my son will be a great man   I have faith that I found the
love of my life   nothing matters in the end but actually, for me, yes,
because I experienced love......

Teresa releases my hand and sprinkles the photograph with my blood. My body feels like a feather, the altar spins, where is the door? I think that is the door. A dim light shines around the door edges. Is this death?

I crawl out the shrine door, and Laura rushes to aid me. A long beep pierces my ears, nothing is audible, but her face speaks a million words.

A shadow stands in front of me with red eyes. My heart races. Who are you? Why do you follow me? I am dead, right? Isn't that what you want? The shadow shifts towards the light; it is Teresa in her white robe spotted with blood.

"Now we are free...." Teresa's ghastly voice echoes in my ears.

Now I can hear Laura's whimpers. But, I am not dead...Yet.

"Love, love, I am ok, I am ok!" I say.

Teresa puts a tight tourniquet around my wounded hand.

"You didn't kill me?"

"All I needed was your blood, not your life."

"You never told me that!"

"Yes, I did. Your father's deeds have been paid for by your blood. That is all this spell needed after 12 years. Santeras do not kill; Oricha teaches us to cure." Teresa says, calm and apathetic.

"How do we know you are not lying?" Laura asks.

"I don't want someone cursed to care for my Joysie. Even the devil cried when he left paradise."

Teresa limps towards the corridor but then loses her balance. A little empathy stirs within me.

"Your faith in love saved you, Rose." Teresa's words parch in her throat.

Laura and I look at each other, the perfect moment for a kiss. Teresa touches her head. She gives a loud grunt and collapses.

"Joysie!" We yell.

Joysie rushes to her aid, pale and clumsy. She shakes her several times…

"Grandma! Grandma!"

Laura moves to check on her, but she does not respond. Teresa is dead.

A dense fog drifts over the pastures. Joysie puts the last drop of dirt on Teresa's tomb. She then places a crucifix made from branches for a tomb marker.

Here lies Teresa Estrada, 8/11/1943– 4/3/2022. RIP.

That is all we can write across the sticks. Joysie drops to her knees and cries. All this evil to avenge her only son and protect her granddaughter is a great show of love… Love gets out of our hands. Love is not always…good. I feel Joysie's pain. It is easy to denounce evil but hard to comprehend it.

Ghastly silhouettes move over the fields. The sun dissipates the fog with casual elegance, and the rays shine across the heavenly pastures and the majestic white mountains. Nature paints this vibrant dream with bird chirps, insect buzzes, roses that smile at me, and a wind that cools my entrails and blows my long hair across the plain. My eyes blink… Pa, Ma, Grams, and Kashmir walk towards me with white garments, barefoot, and with radiant faces. Pa and Kashmir hold hands, Ma has her arm around Grams, and my family smiles at me together for the first time in my life. Joysie, Laura, and Moses turn into granite statues… The perfect contrast of joy and sorrow.

Now it is clear: Life has no solution; life is an experience. There is no eternal pain nor everlasting happiness. When death comes, nothing will matter, only our experience of life. Why hate? Why let norms bind us? Why fear what others think? Why waste life thinking? It is perfectly fine not to understand everything in life. Life is too short to know everything.

There are no conditions for happiness. We must have the courage to find happiness, even in the smallest things. Life exists in our eyes, our eyes only. Nobody can see for us; only we can see the good, the evil, and the unknown… That is true experience. Life and death resolve nothing, but there is nothing to be solved. Love is the only thing that can save us from death. Growing up doesn't mean being absolute; growing up is finding purpose despite our ignorance and even if death is eminent. The best day of our lives is when we decide our purpose, regardless of life's absurdities; only at that moment will we know if we will live or die.

My family waves at me. Hand in hand, they run across the pastures towards two flaming chariots. Joysie's white and black mares pull the chariots up to the sky. The chariots form a beautiful rainbow across the field. A fetus emerges from a rose; it is me! Then I grow into a child, and then as a little girl holding hands with the twins. A grey cloud surrounds me, and now I transform into an older woman that holds hands with a skeleton. We kiss passionately, and wings sprout from my back. I fly over the pastures, laughing, and the skeleton turns to dust. I turn the day into night, and the moon smiles and sucks me into her mouth. The moon melts like molasses over the mountains. The mountains grow and grow… I blink.

We all tell our own stories in our heads, and these stories lead us to find the purpose in our lives. These stories come from our experiences... These stories have what we live for. What is the meaning of my experience? I should not fear death. I should fear not knowing what to truly live for...

The fog thickens, and the temperature drops. Laura covers Moses and heads back to the house, but Joysie remains on her knees, cold and sullen.

"Rose, let's go back to my apartment. We can settle there for now." Laura says.

"We can't leave her here."

Laura looks at her. She then squints and gives me a negative nod.

"She is a fallen angel." Laura says.

The raindrops tickle my skin, and thunder roars across the heavens. We cover Moses from the rain and rush back to the house. Joysie runs behind us.

We place Moses in his car seat, it is a little damp, but at least he will be warm for the ride. Joysie faces the field, absentminded like a statue. I want to bring her with us because she is nothing but a victim. She has no future on this ranch.

She seems innocent, but she will forever see me as a family wrecker. It is easy to pervert a good person, bad things take little effort to learn because we are more prone to evil.

There is no promise between Teresa and I, but it does not feel right to leave an orphan 12-year-old to die. We can be a unique family and transform her sorrow into happiness.

"Laura, we can't leave her here. She will die."

"She is soaked with rain and rancor…I think we should leave her."

"I can't! She risked her life to bring us together." My voice cracks.

Laura grabs my arm as I step out of the car.

"Let her go…."

I stroke Laura's hand, "please, we are lovable people…." She releases my arm. Joysie shivers and turns away from me.

"Joysie, please come with us."

"You hate me, leave…."

"I care for you. I would not be with Laura if it weren't for you."

"This is my home. I promised grandma I would stay here…."

"Don't let the past dictate your future. Come with us. We will be a family, a happy family."

Joysie does not respond. Finally, she turns, wipes her tears, and looks at me with a smirk.

"Will you be my sister?" She asks.

I nod. She hugs me, and I can feel her little heart on my chest. Joysie is not evil, she is just afraid like any other kid. Gullible, confused, and scared, much like me. But it is ok. We are all growing up.

"I promise to love you…. Sister." I say.

We hop into the car. Laura gives her a faint smile. The rain pings angrily against the roof. We should wait for the rain to recede before we leave.

Joysie strokes Moses's head. He giggles, and she kisses his forehead. Not all blessings are good. Some challenge us to see the world in a different way. Other blessings seem good but hurt us when we least expect it, from whom we least expect it. And then there are bad blessings, things that seem bad, take away pleasure, destroy our comfort and purge us from our inner demons. But they transform us to endure life, to endure love, set others free, and realize that our existence is above what the world thinks of us. Moses is my bad blessing.

Joysie stares at Moses. It's hard to decipher her emotion from the retro visor. She then gazes at me through the visor and scowls, her sinister expression shifts to an innocent smile. My curse is a blessing, but I hope our blessings don't turn into a curse…

"Everything ok there?" I ask.

"Yes, Rose… everything ok…." Joysie says.

"Can you please watch him? It is a long drive…."

She nods and touches Moses with both hands. She is an innocent girl, and I think we will get along fine. The rain stops, but the fog lingers. Finally, Laura decides to drive away. My mind swoons as voices bounce in my ears. I dread the moment when I must wake up, but this is reality…right? Yes, that's reality, grow up or suffer for not growing up. Our new family, the wind carries us, the fog obstructs us, we face the future with the happiest haste.

www.ingramcontent.com/pod-product-compliance
Lightning Source LLC
Chambersburg PA
CBHW030529310726
48979CB00010B/1855/J